MIDNIGHT LIMITED

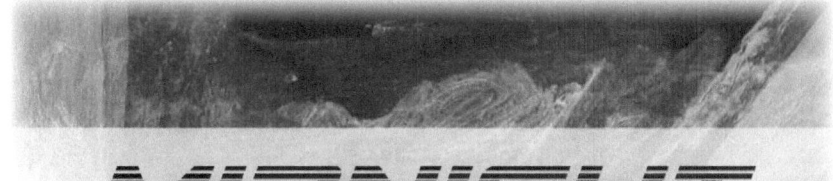

MIDNIGHT LIMITED

11

K. SIMPSON

GSP

GusGus Press • Bedazzled Ink Publishing
Fairfield, California

978-1-949290-32-5 paperback

Cover artwork
by
Rebecca Campbell

Cover Design
by

The following stories appeared in slightly different form in *Late Show & Then Some*
(Bedazzled Ink Publishing, 2015):

B Movie
Fish Shoes
Late Show
Mouse Trap
Prigonometry
Short Form

GusGus Press
a division of
Bedazzled Ink Publishing Company
Fairfield, California
http://www.bedazzledink.com

To those who haunt me

ACKNOWLEDGMENTS

Many thanks to
- Beta readers Shaun Day and Ian Rowan, who've been with me from the first book and made all of them better
- Becky Campbell, who painted the spooky, evocative cover, and Brian Stage, who took the spooky, evocative author photo
- Chuck Hutchinson for the name *Kitty Carlisle* (his own ex-cat) and Shaun Day for the phrase *fish shoes*
- Andrew Simpson and David Finkel for technical details on theater organs
- Sammy Terry, just because

CONTENTS

PROLOGUE
NIGHT TRAIN

THE LATE TRAIN was later than usual, but time mattered nothing to Clara. She liked to ride all night, running the familiar route over and over. The movement was a comfort to her, as it always had been. She could sleep when she was dead. Mostly, she slept in the daytime.

That nice girls didn't ride trains alone at night was immaterial too.

She'd had the pass since she was nineteen. Working in the city had been an adventure then. How miraculous progress still seemed to her—how marvelous that you could leave your quiet, well-groomed country town at eight; step onto a clean, gleaming contraption; and be at your desk in the city by nine.

She had no desk in the city anymore. Her green, pleasant town was an expensive suburb now, one she couldn't afford. Everyone she'd known or loved had gone. She still liked to be where people were, but not *with* them— near enough to see and hear them, to be in the same weather with them, but not to engage. So she rode the train.

Clara shifted by habit as the train picked up speed after a corner. She glanced out the window indifferently, having memorized the view long ago. Her reflection in the dark glass looked the same as always. Tonight, she had on the black coat with the collar turned up. With the black hat, it made a midnight-colored frame for her pretty face. She might have stepped off the cover of *W*, what with the chains, the lacy black gloves, and the clanking brass gadgets all over. This style was in vogue with the young, and she was young enough herself to carry it off. Besides, she'd always looked good in black.

It was too bad that no one was around at the moment to see how well steampunk suited her. There were rumors of a haunted car on this train, and most late-night riders avoided sparsely populated cars in case the rumors were true. Clara might have enlightened them—no ghost had ever approached her—but no one ever asked.

It was unlikely that anyone would ask on this run either. There would be few passengers on this bitter-cold New Year's Day night.

Clara settled back with her memories and stared out the window, unseeing. She was long away and far ago when the train put in at the Stop 11 station and the young people boarded.

She was peripherally aware of them long before she registered them because they were so many, so loud, so insistently alive. They were on their way from one club to another, evidently too high to drive. Clara heard the distant laughter first and then the stomp and clatter and skip of them walking the train, shouting back and forth, searching for the haunted car.

When they finally reached hers, she was staring out the window again.

"Omigod," a girl said. "Look!"

She looked. The young people looked back. They could have been mirrors: pale; beautiful; arrestingly made up; dressed head to foot in high Victoriana trimmed with gears, goggles, and other improbable accessories. One carried a lacy black parasol. Another had black feathers threaded through his long hair. Still others affected watch fobs, top hats and toppers, waxed mustaches, pince-nez. Large, ornate jewelry glittered on vests, bodices, and lapels.

"Omigod," the girl said again (this time to Clara), "where did you get that?"

"Where did I get what?"

The girl slid into the seat across the aisle and leaned over avidly. "*That.*"

Clara touched the mourning brooch on her coat collar. The lovely thing was an antique jet disc trimmed with gold filigree and pearls; in the center, inside a tiny gilded frame, was a man's eye.

"Wicked," said the boy in striped socks.

Clara was perfectly familiar with slang but pretended not to be. "Not very. He's been good company."

"You mean it's a *real person's* eye?" the first girl demanded.

This time, she laughed aloud. It had been a while since she had. "It's only a painting. A miniature. Do you want to see?"

They did. Carefully, she unpinned the brooch and watched them pass it around. While they studied it, she studied them.

One girl in particular caught her attention; the heavy veil concealed the face, but Clara half-recognized something behind it. Some*one*, perhaps; someone she'd known; someone she'd hated. Dimly, a memory stirred. It was hate, then. But who?

She'd almost got there when she noticed the boy standing next to the girl—the boy with the tasseled pink sash that didn't quite suit his severe black clothes, with the dimple and the easy smile. His black hair touched the collar of his coat becomingly. One gloved hand rested on the gilded handle of an ebony walking stick.

He might have been Cyril.

By the time she realized that she was staring at him, she realized that he was staring back. Caught, he moved closer, into the light. He had Cyril's eyes.

"I'm sorry," he told her. "But you look familiar."

"You look familiar too."

He nodded at the vacant seat next to her. "May I?"

She allowed it. His friends left them there.

When the two of them were alone, he pinned her brooch back on her collar. "Amazing coat."

"Thank you."

"Could I see the rest of your costume?"

Obligingly, she unbuttoned the coat and opened it.

HE HADN'T EXPECTED that. Even on New Year's Day night, nice girls didn't ride trains naked. He was mostly sorry that he'd asked.

But the nudity was only the third-to-last thing he'd expected to see under the coat. The next-to-last was the transparency (otherwise concealed by skillfully applied makeup). The very last thing he'd expected was the tattoo, which floated over her transparent chest like a frame of movie film projected on fog. The tattoo was of a face.

His face.

"This is the haunted car," Clara said unnecessarily. "Happy New Year."

He leaped up to run. She leaped and ran with him. When they reached the door, she pulled it open and pushed him out.

"ALL BETTER NOW?" she asked when he returned.

He shook his head experimentally. Then—pale, beautiful, insubstantial— he floated down the aisle and took his seat next to her.

"His name was Cyril," Clara said, touching her brooch again. "We were engaged to be married. He died in the war. And I—"

"Which war?"

What did it matter? Every war was every other war. But he was new, so she humored him.

She told him a version of the story while he listened with mounting dread. The war was the Spanish-American War; Cyril was killed at Kettle Hill in 1898. She tried to join him six weeks later. This train line had been a trolley line then, so it had been easy to jump off a moving car and break her neck. She was still trying to figure out how to die. Life as a phantom, it turned out, was long and mostly uneventful.

"You'll help with that," she said.

"Why me?"

"Why not?"

It didn't matter. Besides, he looked like Cyril, and he already had the clothes.

THEY RODE FOR a while in silence.

"Now what?" he asked.

She laughed without humor. "Bored already?"

"Tell me what happens next."

She couldn't tell him that—ghosts trafficked in the past, mostly, and what would happen next was going to be a surprise—but she had to tell him something. So she told him twenty-two stories.

B MOVIE

Somewhere in the California desert . . .

THEY'D LEFT LA simply hours ago, and the sun was alarmingly low. Soon, it would be dark. Darkness in the desert. Not her idea of a good time. She didn't think it was possible to *have* a good time in a desert. If they didn't get somewhere soon, she'd be calling her agent and canceling this audition. *If* she could get a signal.

That decided, she turned on the driver. "Are we there yet?"

"Almost, baby."

In truth, he didn't know where "there" was, exactly. He'd rented the car with unlimited mileage and no set destination. Then again, he hadn't figured her for the kind who asked questions.

They'd met at a tiny indie festival in Oxnard two weeks ago. Her latest film, *Cannibal Waitresses 2: Sloppy Seconds*, had been indifferently received. But she'd looked like a star on the big screen, with that flame-colored hair and those enormous assets, and he wanted a piece, so he made a point of bumping into her after the screening.

I'm an independent producer, he said.

She yawned.

I'm your biggest fan, he said.

She started to walk away.

I've got a project in development that's perfect for you, he said.

She turned back.

Over many drinks, he spun out his tale. This property was a killer. A couldn't-miss. Guaranteed box-office gold. It would make her the A-lister she'd always deserved to be.

She was listening.

Money? Of course he had the money. A big investor group in Japan was *begging* him to let them finance the picture. Why, the first draw-down amount was due the first of next month.

Distribution? Of course he had distribution. They were fighting over it at Lionsgate and Spyglass right now. His rep was working on an even bigger deal with Warner.

What's it called? she asked.

He ordered another round to stall for time. Finally, he got it. *Hell Motel*, he said. Killer concept. This French guy and this Swedish dame are lost in the desert in the Fifties, and they find this motel. Turns out it's haunted. By a ghost with a chainsaw. Great picture, huh?

She chewed the end of her paper cocktail umbrella, looking almost as though she were thinking. Sex scenes? she asked.

A few, he said. Tasteful as hell.

And you're paying how much again? she asked.

He checked the cocktail napkin on which he'd written the initial figure. Surreptitiously, he edited a digit before he showed her.

Call my agent, she said.

He took the next morning to write a few pages of script before he called her agent. Could she audition for him? Of course she had the part, but the investors wanted some guarantees that she was right for it. To confirm, they'd go to the location and run a few lines. It would be only him and her— no crew yet. He didn't want to inhibit her performance.

Her agent advised against it, but she'd been around long enough to know how B movies got cast. So he'd picked her up late that afternoon, and they'd been driving ever since.

He hoped that there really *was* a motel out this way.

At last, when the sun was only a smudge behind the mountains, they saw the lights ahead. TWILIGHT MOTEL, the sign said in large yellow neon capitals. Below it, small red neon letters flashed V CAN Y.

"We're there, baby," he told her.

HE COULDN'T BELIEVE his luck. The motel was a perfect Fifties time capsule, all pink and turquoise down to the kidney-shaped pool. He half-expected to see tailfin Chryslers and Chevies parked in the lot. He didn't. But he did see a couple of scallop-backed metal lawn chairs outside the office, along with a vintage Pepsi machine.

They *were* there. First the flashback; then the funny business. Perfect!

"Some location, huh?" he asked the woman, who didn't reply. She'd expected dinner.

She waited glumly in the car while he went into the office. For lack of anything else to do, she scanned her lines again. Gawd, they were awful, even for a B movie. She hoped that whoever got cast as Pierre would at least be cute.

THE DESK CLERK was too absorbed in the evening paper to look up when he walked in. "Got a room?" he asked.

There were dumber questions. Not many. Not that this one worked: The clerk continued to not look up.

The man cleared his throat and tapped his foot. He pretended to cough. Finally, he smacked the call bell so hard that the bell went airborne and broke an ashtray (amber glass, just like the ones he remembered from childhood).

That worked.

"We'll try this again," the man said importantly. "Got a room?"

"We have rooms."

The clerk's voice was oddly mechanical, as though he rarely used it, which was possible. The motel was so far out in nowhere that the man (and the woman waiting in the car) might have been his only customers in weeks.

"Got a room with a *big* bed?"

The clerk smiled faintly. "Got ninety bucks?"

Ninety bucks, and he didn't have to buy dinner. Was this a great racket or what?

The clerk took his cash, counted it twice, and lifted a key off a pegboard behind the desk. The key was antique: worn, metal, Yale, chained to a gilded wooden tag. He could barely make out the faded TWILIGHT MOTEL, ROOM 101 stamped into the tag.

"Haven't seen room keys like this since I was a kid," he remarked.

The clerk said nothing.

"What's checkout time?"

"Checkout?"

"Yeah, checkout. The time we leave in the morning. When do we go?"

He didn't see anything particularly funny about the question, but the clerk was still laughing when he went back out to the car.

THE AUDITION FOLLOWED, and later, they slept. So did the desert. No other cars pulled into the motel that night; no traffic passed on the highway.

In the lobby, the desk clerk was still reading the newspaper. There was nothing odd about that in itself, but there was something odd about the paper. Had the man not been in such a rush to audition the woman, he might have noticed the year in the front-page dateline: 1959.

He might also have noticed the second man, who'd been standing outside the office the whole time.

Now that man, dapper in a dark suit and narrow tie, hair shiny and slicked back with tonic, strolled past their room. He paused for a moment to listen; then he walked the few yards to the motel pool. He lit a cigarette. Half in shadow, half in reflected aqua light from the pool, he stood there smoking, watching their door.

THEY GOT UP early. He had to return the car to the rental agency by noon, and she had to get home before her primary boyfriend got back to town. Neither of them said as much, of course; they'd spoken vaguely of urgent business in the city.

"I think that went well," he said, knotting his tie. "I'm satisfied with your performance. I'm sure the investors will be too when I make my report."

She didn't say anything. She'd known since three a.m. that there were no investors and that there was no project, because she'd gone through his wallet and his pockets while he snored like a hog in a bed. Still, the evening had been kind of fun, in a way, and you never knew. If this guy ever *did* turn into a producer, she'd given him reason to remember her.

Misreading her expression, he pulled her close. "Let's have one for the road, baby."

She let him have his fun for a few seconds and then administered a sharp mood-altering honk.

He yelped. "What was *that* for?"

"We're done here. Time to go."

Well, he was ruined for the next few minutes anyhow. "OK, all right, OK. Let me just open the curtains." He wouldn't have ordinarily, but the bill that someone had slipped under the door a few hours ago said this: *On leaving, pull the curtains open for Housekeeping.*

She watched him fumble with the curtain pull; it seemed to be stuck. Idly, she wondered how often Housekeeping came around.

Neither of them noticed the white goo suddenly oozing out of the baseboards.

After a lot more swearing and a little more effort, he wrenched the curtains open. That done, he made for the door. But he didn't get there; somehow, his lead foot was stuck. "Goddamn cheap motel. Carpet's as sticky as a movie-theater floor."

She shrugged. She'd auditioned in worse places.

"I ought to make that jackass clerk refund my—hey! What's that white shit?"

"What white shit?" she asked, incurious.

"On the carpet." He tried to move his back foot, but it was stuck too. "Get over here and help me."

She checked her watch again. Quarter past eight. Damn him, if Johnny got home before she did . . . Well, she'd help this jerk out and then get an Uber back to the city if she had to. That decided, she started across the room.

Then she was stuck herself, and the white goo was all over the carpet, oozing from all the baseboards, running toward the center of the room.

"Let's take our shoes off," she suggested.

They did, after which—unwisely—they tried walking again.

"Fucking motel," he growled. "Can you reach the phone?"

She tried but lost her balance and fell into the goo, which promptly glued her in place, facing away from the window.

For her sake, it was just as well; she couldn't see the shadows that blocked the daylight from the uncurtained window, and she didn't understand why he screamed.

"What's *wrong* with you?" she screamed back.

He couldn't draw breath to answer. He was staring at what was outside staring in at them: two enormous cockroaches, antennae twitching, scaly forelegs tapping the window glass gently. The bigger one held a huge rolled-up newspaper between its next two legs down.

"Oh my God," he whispered.

"Oh my God *what?!?*"

Too bad about what happened next. It would've made a great picture.

YOU CAN'T KEEP A GOOD DOG DOWN

EVERYONE KNOWS THAT cats have nine lives, but it's a little-known fact that dogs have ten. They (whoever they are) say God loves dogs more, which is why they also say all dogs go to heaven.

They don't always get it right, though. Take the strange case of Rover Jones.

Rover was a good dog. He was a smallish terrier mix, black and white and barky, but almost always good. He'd spent his first nine lives faithfully serving his human family, dying and resurrecting discreetly, and his only known vice in those lives (and this last one) was trying to kill the UPS truck.

No one knew what it was about the UPS truck—perhaps the color of the body or the pitch of the engine or the angle of the sun at the hour when the truck made its normal rounds in the neighborhood. It might have been the driver, but the man was so nondescript that you couldn't have picked him out of a police lineup if he'd had three heads and all of them were on fire. The Joneses couldn't imagine how the dog could remember him, much less hate him.

Whatever the cause, whatever the object, Rover remembered and hated with burning, deathless passion. There'd been many situations. Mrs. Jones forgot to latch the front gate sometimes; little Bobby didn't always remember Rover's leash; big sister Sally liked to sic him on people for fun. Mr. Jones, who was a criminal lawyer, used to joke about having a criminal dog, but the joke got less amusing each time the UPS managers called. Lately, the calls had been downright frosty. This last time, Rover came so close to catching the driver that the man lost his left shoe; when Mr. Jones came home from work, the dog was curled up on the big rag rug in the kitchen, eating the leftovers. The shoe was only an ugly brogan and would be cheap to replace, but the homicidal glint in Rover's eye as he gnawed it made Mr. Jones's skin crawl.

"That animal is psychotic," he told his wife that night. "Why, again, are we keeping a psychotic dog?"

Mrs. Jones, busy moisturizing, made noncommittal noises.

"I mean it, Betty. He's no good. He almost took the UPS man's foot off. Can you imagine the lawsuit if he *gets* him next time? With *his* priors?"

"There, there, dear," she said.

"I want you to call the vet first thing in the morning. I want him put down once and for all."

"Who?"

"The *dog*."

"That's nice, dear."

Exasperated, Mr. Jones crossed to her dressing table and took the jar of night cream away.

"Hey!" she cried.

"Did you hear what I just said?"

"Which part?"

When he didn't answer, she made a never-mind gesture. "You don't like the dog. You keep saying it. I've heard this, Don. What do you want *me* to do?"

He told her again.

"Oh, no, I'm not," she said instantly. "I'm not telling the kids we put Rover to sleep. Besides, he's a good boy."

"He's a bad dog."

"Only around UPS trucks."

"Is that so? Do you know what he was doing when I got home? Eating the UPS man's shoe. I swear he was laughing. How do you know he won't turn on *us* next?"

She asked whether there wasn't some medication that he could go back on—"he" in this case being her husband—and the conversation went sharply downhill from there. Sally and Bobby were wide awake in their rooms and heard almost everything. It made Bobby cry, but it gave Sally ideas.

THE NEXT DAY, Mrs. Jones expected a package. It was a present for Mr. Jones, who had a birthday soon, but the present was provisional now.

Little Bobby was in school (good boy!), but Sally was upstairs with what she swore was a cold. Ordinarily, Mrs. Jones would have sent her daughter to school even with bilious fever or tentacles growing out of her forehead, but she was still mad at Mr. Jones and wanted to defy him in every way she could. She'd started by absolutely refusing to call the vet.

As for Rover, he spent most of the day protecting the house (good boy!), vigilant for mice, burglars, space monsters, and cats. In the afternoon, he went to the grocery with Mrs. Jones and waited patiently in the car while she shopped. She bought him a bag of his favorite kibble and some chewy bones. She also bought another bottle of the brownish fluid that Mr. Jones finished last night and something red for herself, with snacks.

A little before three, Sally, lurking in her room, heard her mother's car turn into the driveway. She also heard a large truck pull up to a curb down the block.

It was the work of a moment for the girl to scramble downstairs to open the front door for Rover. She'd opened the front gate herself while her mother was out.

IT WAS TOO bad, Mr. Jones told the children later. It was a shame that the UPS truck ran over Rover. But it wasn't the driver's fault. He hadn't been *aiming* at the dog.

(He had been.)

They could get a new dog soon, Mrs. Jones promised. Maybe a nice poodle.

Mr. Jones' expression darkened.

Well, *something* nice, Mrs. Jones said.

Bobby was inconsolable, however. He'd wept and raged at the cruelty of fate since he'd come home from school and heard the news, and the further news that Animal Control would be coming for the remains soon only made things worse. He held his breath, refused to eat supper, whined, kicked a chair leg, threw peas at his sister, and generally made family life so unpleasant that Mr. Jones finally agreed to bury the dog in the back yard.

After supper, Mr. Jones took a long-handled spade out of the garden shed and dug a shallow hole near the back fence by flashlight. Then he fetched Rover's body (wrapped in an old beach towel) from the garage and dropped it into the hole, towel and all.

Bobby stayed to watch his father shovel dirt back into the grave. Even after everyone else went inside to make popcorn, he stayed behind to bargain.

He was a good dog, the boy prayed. *He was really, really good. Do good dogs* have *to go to heaven?*

WHEN THE JONESES came downstairs the next morning, Rover was waiting at the bottom of the staircase, wagging his tail. Mrs. Jones fainted.

Heart pounding like a piston, wanting to faint himself but not in front of the children, Mr. Jones ran to check the back yard. The grave was still there. But the ground had been disturbed, and the dirty beach towel was unwrapped.

The family agreed not to say a word to anyone. Then, thoroughly spooked, they went off to work, bridge, and school.

That afternoon, Rover got run over by the UPS truck again. Mr. Jones reburied him in the backyard grave (digging it deeper first), and as before, Bobby stayed after to weep and pray.

THIS HAPPENED FIVE more times. By the third time, even Bobby was getting bored. Still, the dog kept coming back: squished by three, buried by eight, reconstituted by seven. You could set your watch.

Finally, Rover himself was done with it. He'd been a very good boy in all ten lives. No one had said anything about do-overs. He was supposed to go to heaven—not keep getting resurrected in Pasadena. He wasn't having it anymore.

On the seventh morning, when the Joneses came downstairs to find him alive again, he ate them. A few hours later, he ate the UPS driver. Then he ran off with a cute Maltese from Glendale. *That* was more like it. Good dogs go to heaven, but bad dogs go everywhere.

OUTSOURCED

WHIZBANG! & CO., Inc., turned 100 on a Halloween day and took itself private to celebrate. The huge publishing conglomerate had vanquished the last of its foes the previous year, thanks to a successful campaign of low-price-gouging, dirty tricks, extortion, and a couple of quiet murders; its flagship Whizbangs! books ruled the self-help category alone. Even nonreaders bought Whizbangs!, which were sold everywhere now and awarded free with enough fuel points at the major gas-station chains. The famous red-and-white covers with the firecracker logo were everywhere. The books were as unavoidable as death, as hurtful as taxes, roughly as helpful as flu, but they sold and sold and sold.

It was a pity that so many Americans were in need of so much self-help. But Whizbang! & Co. was not in the business of mercy.

Its recent success was the work of the corporation's new chairman, president, and CEO, Vince Pritchard. The board had lured him off Wall Street, where he'd personally driven six midsize cities into bankruptcy and wiped out the savings of thousands of teachers, firefighters, police officers, and other civil servants who offended by drawing government paychecks. He demanded, and got, a package the size of a small country's budget, which the board funded by selling a few minor imprints. This sale cost a couple hundred jobs, but across the corporation, individual jobs didn't matter, not even a couple hundred. Even the loss of Whizbang!'s current top executives was irrelevant; the new CPCEO was bringing in a hand-picked team to help him lead the company to ever-greater heights.

The day Pritchard took over at Whizbang!, the stock (WZB) rose 15 percent. The day after, Pritchard put two more imprints on the block—two of the corporation's most-respected. When both imprints sold (at fire-sale prices), a hundred more employees were put out of work. Whizbang! shares soared.

Pritchard and his lieutenants exercised all their options, buying, selling, splitting, and shorting whatever they could, leaving the publishing operation to run itself. When the board expressed mild uncertainty about this strategy, Pritchard agreed to hire consultants.

BEING AN EDITOR for Whizbang! had never been easy. First off, there was the embarrassment factor, which was large. The company was headquartered in the backwater Plains, far from the glamour of Manhattan, and its name and logo were so profoundly uncool that even backwater Plainsmen made fun of them. Then there was the quality of the product, which was dismal at best. Whizbangs! were written (the company preferred "authored") by subject-matter experts who couldn't write and in too many cases weren't experts on their subjects either but who happened to know a friend of an acquisitions editor or who'd had too many drinks with one at a trade show. Further, there was the absence of craft in the work. At Whizbang!, the author was law; editors were allowed only to fix punctuation and make a few invisible passes over structure. ("This policy preserves the integrity of the Authorial vision," the editorial guidelines said, "and removes interfering editorial barriers between Author and reader.")

Lilith Hart was grateful for the job all the same. She'd bounced around publishing for most of her working life, never making much but never minding much either. She wasn't ambitious, the way so many of her classmates had been, and she was too literate to stick in some of the better-paid jobs she'd tried. Until a friend hired on at Whizbang!, she'd been working a temp job at a big insurance company, answering some pompous executive's phones. The friend helped her get freelance work at Whizbang! at first and then his own job when he left.

"Whizbang!'s not what you think, Lily," Todd warned her one day at lunch. "It's not publishing. It's a factory. It makes one thing: It makes people *sick*."

"Is this a test?" Lilith asked, laughing. "I thought I already had the job."

He smiled grimly and told her more war stories. She listened politely, making sympathetic noises at the right times to prove she was paying attention. But honestly—Todd had always been high-strung. He got too wrapped up in his work, took it too seriously, and took setbacks too hard. His new job at a not-for-profit would suit him much better than work in the tough, competitive private sector. As for her, she was a survivor. She'd be fine. She was just happy to have a real editing job again.

TWO MONTHS INTO that job, Lilith saw a colleague taken out of an editorial meeting on a gurney. She'd never seen a nervous breakdown before; she'd never really believed in any such thing. But the paramedics who came to take Megan to the hospital seemed to be grimly familiar with the routine. Afterward, in the break room, a senior editorial assistant whispered to her that this was the third breakdown so far this year and that none of the other broken had come back to work.

Lilith called Todd that night. He advised her to find the managing editor's assistant the next day and get in on the pool.

By that time, Vince Pritchard had been the head man at Whizbang! for less than a year.

NEXT, THE CONSULTANTS came.

Snatchley, Grabber, Skeevy, & Dix Consulting Group had helped Pritchard with some of his most profitable deals in his investment-banking days, so he turned to them for help with his Whizbang! schemes. Profits and share prices were up sharply, but Pritchard felt sure that there was even more profit to be squeezed out. After all, Whizbangs! were the undisputed market leaders in all the self-help categories, from car repair to cooking to brain care, and there was always more money to be made from a market leader.

Pritchard and his lieutenants (called publishers now) rented the ballroom at a hotel up the road from Whizbang! headquarters for a mandatory all-company meeting on the first day of the new fiscal year, which was November 1. Satellite offices around the world watched by . . . well, satellite. The CPCEO announced the new partnership with SGSD to find further operating efficiencies and expressed his expectation of cooperation from every employee.

THE CONSULTANTS WERE still on the job six months later. Few employees at Lilith's level ever saw them except from a distance, scurrying into elevators or scuttling down hallways, but there was no mistaking them. Except for the ten men of uppermost management—Pritchard and the publishers—they were the only people in the building who wore suits to work, and they took their briefcases everywhere, even (it was said) to the men's room.

No word leaked out about what the consultants were up to, but the rumor mill ground overtime. Some people heard that the whole production department would be outsourced, which was nonsense. Others insisted that everyone who made more than $40,000 a year and/or had four years of service would be let go, which was hogwash. But a few odd things were happening:

- Several senior members of staff and one department head announced their plans to retire at the end of the quarter. Quarter-end was a month away, so the jobs would need filling promptly. They went unfilled.
- In a few departments, senior employees were demoted to work under junior ones straight out of college.
- The freelancers were starting to complain of trouble getting paid, and the ones who had the most trouble also seemed to have the hardest time getting new assignments.
- Coffee was no longer complimentary (but employees could pay $10 a week to a coffee fund if they chose to), and there would be no more free paper clips, staples, sticky notes, and pens.

Everyone ignored the part about the office supplies. They paid attention to the part about benefit cuts, though. "Your management is making these cuts reluctantly," Pritchard said in the memo, "in an effort to save jobs." It may have been mere coincidence that Whizbang!'s stock went up so much the following day.

On a day-to-day level, Lilith's work was unaffected. She was coping better than many of the longtime editors on staff; years of freelancing and temping had taught her not to expect much. While her colleagues fretted and gossiped and wrote mean jokey social-media posts about the consultants, she kept her head down and worked.

She also watched. The already-low quality of the manuscripts was getting lower all the time—so bad now that editors were starting to use the fake names on their books' mastheads. At the same time, title count was dropping. Lately, she'd been saving the weekly production schedules, and she noticed that books were steadily dropping off the schedule—not many at a time, but a substantial number over months. The editors of those books shrugged and accepted reassignment quietly, for the most part. The ones who didn't had a funny way of being let go or going on medical leave.

Lilith noticed, too, that the ones who took leave didn't come back. She won $23 in the office pool when a certain excitable indexer left.

JUST BEFORE FIVE on a Friday afternoon, the production department was let go. There was no warning—only a red-flagged memo that read as follows:

> In an effort to streamline operations and realize greater efficiencies, on the advice of SGSD Consulting Group, your management has partnered with KMA Services in Bangalore, India, which will provide all production services for Whizbang! titles effective two weeks from today. We know that you join us in welcoming KMA to the Whizbang! family and look forward to many successful years of close cooperation.

Lilith's cubicle was down the hall from the production department—the large open area where the compositors, proofreaders, and artists worked. She knew all of them. Crumpling the memo (she wouldn't give the bosses the satisfaction of earning a fraction of a penny on recycling it), she went to production to offer her sympathy.

The head of Illustration was wandering the aisles, looking lost. When Lilith approached, he wiped his eyes. "They asked me to go to Bangalore to train my replacement," he said. "They offered me two more weeks of employment and half off the airfare."

Heartsick, she watched him wipe his eyes again. "What did you say?"

"What *could* I say? I have a family and a mortgage. Two more weeks of a paycheck is two more weeks of paying the bills."

"But training your *replacement* . . . ?"

"I'm sixty years old, Lily. This may be the best offer I get now."

She went back to her cubicle after she went to the women's room to cry. Mostly for him, partly for herself.

THINGS AFTER THAT happened quickly. Satellite offices around the world started closing on a Monday; all were dark by the following Friday. Department heads toppled like dominoes. Marketing and most of Human Resources disappeared. Soon, individual employees followed, starting with those who made more than $40,000 a year and/or had four years of service. (Five years meant a fully vested pension.)

Proofreading went to India the first week of August, followed by copyediting. Both department heads were offered trips to Chennai to train their successors, but both refused. Security—since when did Whizbang! have security?—instantly removed them from the building.

That time, at least, project and development editors who fell below income and seniority limits were passed over. Someone with Whizbang! experience had to check the offshore vendors' work, and there were fewer employees all the time who had Whizbang! experience, let alone any publishing experience at all.

By the end of the company's fiscal year, more employees had been laid off, and more work outsourced, than in the previous ten years combined. Pritchard and his publishers drew enormous bonuses. As an extra reward for their stellar work, the board installed an executive helipad.

WHIZBANG! & CO.'S imposing headquarters building was mostly leased to other companies a few months later. Only the ten top executives (Pritchard and his publishers) remained, with virtual assistants in Mumbai handling their administrative tasks. There'd been room on the top floor to build suites for all ten execs, plus a few nice offices for the consultants, along with a private elevator to the rooftop executive helipad.

All the editors who had once worked in-house were gone. A few still freelanced for Whizbang!, but only when the offshore vendors got busy and needed to outsource work. The freelancers worked for less than a third of their former rate. Payment was made on completion of projects, which often ran months late and was supposed to be made in ninety days but often took longer.

Lilith was one of the freelancers. She was in her late fifties now, invisible to most employers and undesirable to all, and the only thing she'd ever been good at was editing. But Whizbang! was the only publisher of any size in the region, and the few available editorial jobs had long since been snapped up by younger, cheaper temps. She had a sick mother and couldn't leave for greener pastures (assuming that there were any for her), so she did the best she could with freelancing for Whizbang! and working odd jobs whenever she had to.

By August, Lilith's income was less than a third what it had been the year before. She discovered, to her dismay, that she was eligible for food stamps, Medicaid, and the local food pantry.

She was lucky at that. The local newspaper and TV stations had been silent while all the layoffs were going on—one didn't cross a well-known international company with powerful directors—but now they were beginning to cover some of the fallout. A few of the longest-laid-off employees, unable to find new work, had fallen into poverty. Downtown, near the river, publishing camps were springing up under bridges. Many of the inhabitants used pages from Whizbangs! to patch holes in their tents and their clothes and their shoes.

AT THE VERY top of the Whizbang! building, if they'd had to patch anything, they'd have used stock certificates. The company was wildly, obscenely profitable thanks to the consultants' advice and the executives' avarice. Sponsoring those reality TV shows alone was worth a fortune; *Whizbang!'s Housewife Deathmatch* was No. 1 on cable. The naked-cooking and extreme-ski-fighting shows were rating well too. All the stars were signed to lucrative contracts for their own Whizbangs! (written by offshore ghostwriters), which sold and sold and sold.

The books themselves didn't matter. They never *had* mattered, but they counted for less than nothing now. CPCEO Pritchard got the brilliant idea to crowdsource books, and it was like getting yet another license to print money. For absolutely no author costs and rock-bottom editorial, production, and marketing costs, Whizbang! was making massive profits on the hottest publishing phenomenon in America.

Pritchard appeared on TV newsmagazines and print-magazine covers. One influential business writer called him "the genius breathing new life into a familiar brand" (and got his own contract for a Whizbang!). There was no cloud on the company's horizon.

Until Lilith bought the book.

SHE HADN'T INTENDED to. Money was desperately tight that month, and she was already worried that the latest past-due check wouldn't come in time to keep the lights on. Her sick mother had passed away over the summer, leaving her a few family heirlooms and several debts; she was trying to pay the latter without selling the former.

On that early-September afternoon, she'd walked to the grocery for a loaf of bread. The car had a quarter-tank of gas, too little to waste, and the weather was still warm enough to make the walk fairly pleasant. She counted her money again on the way to make sure she had enough.

The last thing she expected to see at the store was a Whizbangs! display, but there it was, right inside the front door. It was the kind that the company used to set up at bookstores (before most of the bookstores closed), offering a dozen or so titles with the familiar colorful covers and the promise "Hard Stuff Made Easy." The title that caught her eye was an odd one: *Whizbang!'s How to Be a Witch.*

Lilith didn't have enough money to buy it but made careful note of the price (which had gone up considerably in the past year). Two weeks later, after skipping several meals and a phone bill, she walked back to make the purchase.

ODD THINGS BEGAN to happen shortly thereafter. The Monday night of the first week of October, an SGSD consultant called the police from a Whizbang! suite. Something was in his office, he insisted, breathing on him and laughing. The patrolmen who answered the call found no evidence of pranking; they advised him to go home and sleep it off.

A day later, an unsigned, unpostmarked note arrived for him in the mail: **You will be outsourced.**

The consultant showed it to his supervisor, who showed it to one of the publishers, who showed it to the boss. "Nuts," Pritchard said.

That evening, the consultant fell down the shaft of Whizbang!'s private elevator. It was a long fall. Not much survived but his shoes.

Wednesday morning, a note arrived for the dead consultant's supervisor: **You will be outsourced.**

"Bull," the supervisor said, crumpling it and tossing it into a recycling bin. The rotor of the company helicopter chopped his head off that afternoon.

The notes arrived every few days after that. Neither the postal inspectors nor the police could explain how they wound up in regular U.S. mail, but they came all the same—past Whizbang!'s extra lobby security, past the armed private-elevator attendant, past the bulletproof glass of the executive suite and its many guards. All were followed by lurid, damaging events.

One consultant was boiled in hog fat, in an iron cauldron that somehow got into his office. Another was eaten (mostly) by his own briefcase. Pritchard's top publisher broke out in massive eruptions of rubles, marks, and yuan; the yuan were the ones that eventually suffocated him.

"Balls," Pritchard said.

On the last day of the fiscal year, October 31, the final note arrived, addressed to CPCEO Pritchard himself:

You will be outsourced.

He laughed defiantly. It echoed. The executive floor was empty now except for him.

At the end of the day, several sheriff's deputies, two state troopers, and a private security guard escorted him from the building to his armor-plated limo. Before he got in, Pritchard passed around some of his fine Cuban cigars. "Trick or treat," he said. "See you tomorrow, boys."

THERE WAS NO tomorrow for Vince Pritchard. He never appeared at Whizbang! & Co. headquarters again. But eventually, he turned up here and there.

His liver was outsourced to Chennai, packed in a box of copies of *Whizbang!'s How to Be Best at Business*. His spleen went to Bangalore; his pancreas, to Jaipur. A while later, his brain appeared in Delhi; it was a tiny, shriveled thing of no use to anyone, and it burned black in the fire with the rest of the trash. No one ever found his heart, but it had been a rumor anyway.

KYLIX

SOMETHING IN THE night air intoxicated her, not the usual street-fair smells, not a smell at all so much as a mysterious sense. Amy had a good nose for mystery. Years ago, in the Athenian agora, she'd been enchanted by the scent of an ancient olive tree where there was no tree, marvelous to her but undetectable to her friends, who said she was crazy. She didn't have those friends anymore. Not since she married him. Not since he died.

Had it really been almost a year?

Some details were already fading. She hadn't touched wine since she'd lost him, not a drop of anything, but clarity hadn't kept him with her. She was already forgetting the most intimately familiar things. That morning, she'd passed his aftershave on the street and forgotten that it was his until half a block later. She was too young to forget, too young to be a widow, much too young (and still lovely) to be alone in a festival crowd on a warm, clear September night.

He'd always loved the Greek Festival. They'd always gone there together. That was why she was there now.

She gazed into the wine-dark sky, wondering whether he knew.

No sooner did she wonder than he seemed to answer. For a few heartbeats, she felt him with her. It had been months since she'd felt him at all, even as memory. But this was real—the real Alan, the man himself. She actually smelled that aftershave, his brand of toothpaste, the soap he used in the shower. She drew a deep breath of him, closed her eyes, leaned in.

A young male voice swore violently and shoved her off.

She opened her eyes in time to see the boy she'd accidentally leaned into make a vulgar gesture as he walked away. His friends sneered over their shoulders at her. This was fine behavior for a festival on the grounds of a proper Greek Orthodox church where no alcohol was allowed (but a thin stream of liquor fumes trailed them all the same).

While she stood in the festival street, wondering what to do, an older man bumped her in passing. Then a young couple did. They were in no hurry to get anywhere; they were simply careless. They were happy. They were young, alive, and together.

Maybe this hadn't been such a good idea.

She was turning to leave when she saw the beautiful thing among the knickknacky junk on a long table in the bazaar tent. It sat there patiently, waiting. It seemed to be waiting for her.

THE WOMAN AT the bazaar table didn't know where the object had come from. Some antiques shop might have had it once, she said; it could have been in an estate sale. She'd bought the lot and asked no questions.

Amy held it up to the glare of the string lights for a better look. The beautiful thing was a kylix—the broad, shallow drinking cup of ancient Greece, to all intents and purposes a saucer with handles. It might have been ancient itself or the recent work of a forger. Whatever made it gleam like beaten gold was only a pottery glaze. But what had first caught her eye still held it: the amethysts set in the handles.

She was born in February. Amethyst birthstone. She was legally named for it. "Amy" was short for it. The first gift Alan ever gave her was the violet crystal on a chain; it reminded him of her eyes, he said.

Absorbed, she turned the vessel around and around, studying it from all angles. She'd seen many like it in museums, and the outer decoration seemed to be ordinary and genuine enough. The painting on the bottom, however, was neither. It depicted the usual drinking-and-revelry scene, but with only two dancers.

She was one of them. That was her own face at the bottom of the cup, accurate to the tiniest detail, as clear as a photo taken that moment where she stood.

The other dancer wasn't Alan.

"How much?" she asked after a long time.

The woman told her. The price was too high, but Amy paid it before the woman could change her mind.

As she walked away from the bazaar table, something in the kylix flashed. The empty cup was brim-full of wine.

SHE TOOK HER purchase behind one of the church's olive trees, grown from cuttings brought over from the Old Country. The tree shaded her from the electric lights of the festival but admitted moonshine. As she gazed into the cup, the moon seemed to dance in the dark fluid that filled it.

Over by the lamb spits, the Syrtos was about to start again. Someone was playing a bouzouki, joined by what sounded to her ear like laoutos, slightly out of tune. It never occurred to her to wonder how she knew what laoutos were.

Neither did it dawn on her right away that the tree she was standing next to smelled like the invisible one in Athens all those years ago. She'd felt then, as now, that it was sense memory from another life, a happier life in a world now as dead as—

"Dionysus," she said aloud. She poured a libation for the god before she put the kylix to her lips.

The wine was the best she'd ever tried, so she tried again. Not till the third trial did fog start rising from the ground where she'd poured for the god.

Somehow, she knew what would happen before it did. She watched without surprise or fear as the fog swirled, thickened, lengthened, took on form and mass, and when he stepped from it, she knew him. He was the man at the bottom of the kylix. He wasn't Alan.

That he was naked was a detail. That was only part of his surpassing beauty, from his shining curls to his sculpted torso to the white of his smile. She felt naked herself somehow in the face of him, so she waited to see what would happen.

What happened was that he spoke. He shouldn't have.

"I must have died and gone to heaven," he said, "because you must be an angel. Buy you another drink, doll?"

She was halfway to the festival street when he pulled her back. "Was it something I said? Already?"

"I thought you were a god," she said. "Not some sleazy pickup artist."

He laughed, not unkindly. "And I thought you'd read your *Bulfinch's*. What did you think goes on at Olympus? Parcheesi? Tiddlywinks? Leapfrog?"

"I know about the sex. But—"

"But nothing. Zeus did Leda as a swan for weeks, you know. All I'm looking for is one night. No feathers. I'm a *modern* god." That smile again. "You know you want to."

Did she? He was perfectly, hurtfully gorgeous—it actually hurt to look at him—and nothing about him was like her late husband. It would be betrayal. It would be shame.

—It would be as soon as she could get him behind the olive tree.

They embraced. More happened next. He set the kylix within reach on the ground, and they both drank from it. Amy drank to the bottom.

"Hey, you weren't supposed to—"

She touched the tip of her index finger to his lips. "Later."

THE AUDIENCE WAS chanting "*Opa!*" and throwing coins to the dancers by the lamb spits when Amy rejoined the party. She was no longer quite herself. Something new—and ancient—flickered behind her amethyst eyes. In her left hand was what was left of the kylix.

For the rest of the evening, she was the life and soul of the festival.

The police never found the boy who had shoved her earlier—only something charred and parts of his Nikes.

FISH SHOES

AT LONG LAST, the goldfish were asleep. Gary checked again through the curved part of the bowl—the part that magnified—to make sure. Their bright scaly chests rose and fell with perfect regularity; their shiny tails fluttered gently in the current; their glassy eyes were closed tight. As he did in the evenings, Bubbles had dozed off in his armchair with the newspaper open over his chest to the sports page. Likewise, as was her custom, Goldie was conked out on the loveseat next to the radio, which was still playing.

"They're out," Gary reported. "I say we go tonight."

The woman with whom he shared the bowl looked skeptical but said nothing.

"Now or never, Diane. They're out. Tonight's the night."

"If you say so," she said. "Not that *I* have any say in it. Just keep your voice down, would you? They'll hear you."

He was already rummaging in his dive bag for the tools. "I told you, they're asleep. The time to worry is—"

"The time to *worry* was before we went on that stupid scuba trip in the *first* place. This is *your* fault."

"This again?"

No answer. He glanced up. Yes, she was still mad. Of course she was.

"C'mon, honey, we don't have time for this now. Would you bring me the air hose, please?"

Spitefully, she feigned ignorance. "Which one?"

There was only the one air hose in the bowl. It brought the air in. He waited.

"Oh, all right, here's your stupid hose." She popped it out of the plastic clips that secured it to the flat side of the bowl but let it dangle. "I *wanted* to stay at the hotel and have Mai-Tais by the pool, you know. There were palm trees and everything. We could have gone to the spa later. We could have had couples massage. It was our *anniversary*."

"I know, dear; I was there. Will you bring me the hose? I'm going to need a little extra oxygen while I'm working."

Coolly, she parked herself on a ceramic coral and pretended to ignore him, but she secretly watched him go fetch the hose himself, sliding awkwardly over the flawed glass at the bottom of the bowl. If he fell and broke a leg or his big fat head, she might never get back to Maui.

For once that vacation, luck was on her side: Gary got across the bowl and back in one piece. For safekeeping, he wedged the end of the hose between two towers of the ceramic castle. "Come help me empty the treasure chest, at least," he told the woman.

"You do it. I might break a nail. Not that *you'd* care, but I spent all morning the other morning getting my nails done. Did you notice? No. Do you *ever* notice? No."

"Do you ever give it a rest? We're on vacation."

"And we've spent most of it here, thanks to you and your brilliant ideas." For emphasis, she kicked the fake coral. "Where the hell *is* here?"

Gary asked himself the same question often but never got a satisfying answer. One minute on Wednesday, they'd been diving in sunlit blue water, surrounded by Technicolor fish; the next, they were caught in a net that hadn't been there the minute before. Everything went black, and when they woke, here they were. Wherever "here" was. Reckoning by his scuba watch, it was Friday, so they'd been in the bowl for three days—long enough for him to study their captors, learn their ways, and work out an escape plan.

At least the giant goldfish had been kind to them so far. He and Diane got plenty of food (bran flakes tipped into the bowl, but better than no food). The fish kept their bowl clean, changed their water as needed, and added a few new toys every day. One of those toys was the treasure chest, which had given Gary the idea.

"Yada yada," he said. "Divorce me when we're back on land. If I don't divorce you first. Now *help* me here, already."

AFTER A GOOD hour of effort, which involved most of the tools in Gary's dive bag and chipped a nail on Diane, the escape pod was ready. Together, they'd tipped the plastic treasure chest over to dump out the plastic loot. Then she watched while he cut holes in the treasure chest's lid with his scuba knife and jerry-rigged a pulley out of bits and pieces of scrap from his bag, including old scuba hose, bungee cords, and duct tape.

They'd argued a while about whether the rig would work. It might, it might not, but if Gary was right, it wouldn't have to work long. When they were out of the bowl and back in the water, the current would take them to open ocean, where they'd resurface. They should have just enough air in their scuba tanks to breathe until then.

"What if it *doesn't* work?" she asked for the fourth time.

"I've told you and *told* you, there's no point asking. We've got this one shot. Sue me if it doesn't work."

"It had *better* work. You're *supposed* to know what you're doing, Mr. Big-Shot Engineer, Mr. Let's Go Scuba Diving on Our Tenth Anniversary. Do you know what my mother says about you?"

"Divorce!" Gary snapped, fastening his second flipper. "The *second* we get topside! I can't *wait* to get shot of you, woman. Now put your gear on, and get in the escape pod."

"No."

"What do you mean, 'no'? We're going. Get in."

"Not until you apologize."

"For what?"

She made a very rude face. "You *know* what."

"No, I don't."

"You do."

"I do not. Don't make me, Diane."

"Make you what?"

Gary swept her off her feet and threw her into the treasure chest. She landed awkwardly, breaking the nail she'd chipped earlier. He offered no sympathy. Then he got in after her and pulled on the cord of the makeshift pulley. Slowly, surely, the treasure chest began to climb. "Put on your scuba mask at least," he said.

"Quit bossing me, Gary."

"There's nothing to breathe at the top of the bowl, but suit yourself. *Save* me the divorce fee and drown."

She called him a few choice things. He called her a few back. She told him what her mother said about him. He told her what her mother could do, with what power tools. The bickering went on throughout their slow ascent.

They were nearly there when Diane screamed. The surprise made Gary lose his grip on the pulley cord, sending the treasure chest crashing back to the bottom of the bowl.

Bubbles and Goldie were no longer asleep across the room. They were wide awake, swimming in place by the bowl, peering in. On her fins, the female balanced a large bamboo tray set with small plates, fish knives, and a tube of wasabi.

The male's lips moved, almost as though he were speaking. The humans in the bowl didn't understand him, but Goldie did. She put down the tray and offered him a person-size net.

MOUSE TRAP

AFTER THREE WEEKS of it, Geraldine was sure she would go insane. Night after night, she'd been hearing these *noises* under her bedroom floor—scurrying, scritching, panic-inducing noises that could only mean mice. She'd tried everything: snap traps, glue traps, cheese bait, peanut butter, poison. Every night, she moved the traps, hoping to fool the filthy pests; every morning, she found the traps intact.

The night finally came when the noises were inside her bedroom walls, directly behind her headboard. She spent the rest of the dark hours on the couch with a carving knife and called an exterminator the instant his office opened. He inspected her house that afternoon.

"It's mice all right, lady," he said. "Want me to take 'em out for you?"

She did. She followed him to the back yard, watched him wriggle into the crawl space, and waited anxiously until he reemerged.

The exterminator promised that her worries were over. He'd laid traps and poison at strategic points along the foundation. In a few days, he'd come back to collect the dead and rebait the traps for survivors. Grateful, Geraldine wrote a check.

MORE WHITE NIGHTS followed, all of them alive with mice. The day the exterminator returned to check the crawl space was not a minute too soon.

"Got most of 'em, looks like," he told Geraldine. "We'll do traps and poison again and see what happens by Monday."

She wrote another check.

MONDAY CAME. GERALDINE, half-dead on her feet from lack of sleep, answered the doorbell at the first ring. Cheerfully, the exterminator reported that he'd just come from the crawl space, and the mice were no more. He'd just plug the holes in the foundation for her, and she'd be good to go.

Geraldine, alarmed, asked him what holes in the foundation.

"Oh, it don't take much," he said. "A mouse can get in a house through a hole as big as a dime."

This failed to comfort her. She wrote another check.

SHE WAS WAITING on the front porch in her nightgown when the exterminator came back the following night. He was on 24-hour emergency rates now, but it *was* an emergency.

She paced back and forth, back and forth in the kitchen while he checked the crawl space.

"Nothing," the exterminator said.

That was impossible; she was still hearing mice.

"Then you've got ghost mice, lady," he told her, "because I surely killed 'em all."

Still chuckling at his own wit, he bent over the invoice pad on the counter and started writing. Geraldine crept up behind him with the cast-iron skillet.

FOR THE REST of that night, there were new noises under her bedroom floor: thumping, pounding, swearing, pleading, occasional hysterical laughter. She slept through all of it, smiling. The hard part had been dragging the unconscious body to the back yard and rolling it into the crawl space; next-hardest was sealing the hatch. The labor had been heavy, and it had tired her out.

Geraldine thought she loved all God's creatures but mice, but she had no qualms about what she'd done. The noises down below would stop soon, and when they did, her troubles would be over.

The ghost mice were doomed. Soon, she'd have a ghost exterminator. Better yet, he'd work for free.

PRIGONOMETRY

DON KIRBY HATED Fridays the way you hate Mondays. Weekends were torment for him: no geometry to teach, no young minds to mold or send to detention. He lived for his weekdays in Room 309. Chalk dust, protractors, and compasses were the stuff of his dreams. On a good day, he might spring pop quizzes on all his classes; on a bad one, he might lecture on the philosophy of Platonic solids. Older students and veteran members of faculty had vivid memories of Dodecahedron Week, which still burned in infamy.

No one liked Mr. Kirby.

If you'd asked him, though, and if he'd been the kind of person who noticed or cared, he'd have told you that popularity is cheap.

HE WAS BORN a Donovan—named for some pot-smoking Sixties hippie-freak folk singer who sang about the color yellow—and reared in liberal conditions over his parents' art gallery. Literally over: The whole downstairs of the house was gallery and studio, with the studio frequently spilling over to the back yard, especially when his mother was working on a sculpture garden. Little Donovan found it hard to explain some of the more abstract pieces to his playmates. The crash-test dummy wrapped in an American flag, wearing a Governor Reagan Halloween mask, was only part of an installation that his mother was calling *Dog Bless America*, but that single part had sent a schoolmate home in tears. She was a girl he liked.

"It's a metaphor, sweetie," his mother told him later, when he complained. "It's art."

Then there'd been *Gas Hog*: the front half of a '67 Chevy Camaro Z/28 with fat racing stripes bolted to the back half of a huge pink plaster pig. This was bad enough all by itself, but then there was the grille, which had been pried apart and reshaped into a snarling mouth with bloody metal fangs. He'd hated that part even more. The mean face faced his bedroom window the whole time his parents were working on the piece, and at night, the next-door neighbors' security light painted scary shadows on it. Both his friends refused to come over to play until the thing was gone. They stopped talking to him at school for good measure, in case any of it had been his idea.

"Art isn't always safe, son," his father said. "Sometimes you have to shake people up to get them to *see*."

It went like that for years, from sandbox to SATs. Little Donovan seethed with secret rage in art classes, found sanctuary in math, and never wondered whether he hated his parents. The boy who couldn't draw, paint, or sculpt grew into a man who no longer cared. His parents liked his brother better anyway.

After graduation, Donovan changed his first name to Donald and took a teaching job far from California. The Midwest was a good fit for him. Teaching high school geometry suited him. Abstractions were for escapists; art was for dreamers. The only lines he liked were straight ones, running parallel into infinity. Geometry never changed. You could count on that.

ON THE DAY in question, Mr. Kirby was in his twenty-sixth year of teaching at Hoover High and was essentially the same man he'd been in the first. He still wore only white button-down shirts with conservatively striped ties (red or blue, not too skinny or wide). All his socks were navy blue to go with his pants except the pair that went with the black dress suit. All his shoes were oxblood wingtips. He'd had Richard Nixon's hair for a couple of decades.

The students were different nowadays, though. Pythagoras's ghost, they were different. The clothes they wore, the music they liked, their language— everything about them exceeded the bounds of reason. Further, they were insolent to a degree that begged to be punished. One day early in the school year, before the bell rang to start third period, he heard two students talking outside his classroom door.

"Gotta go, bro," one of them said. "I've got prigonometry."

The other one laughed insultingly hard and yelled it to another student, who also laughed and passed it on, and so on down the hall.

Mr. Kirby spent the first few minutes of that class on lexicology— not his subject but not impertinent. This course, he reminded his pupils, was geometry. Geometry encompassed but was not itself trigonometry. Trigonometry was the body of knowledge of triangles and trigonometric functions and their applications. Prigonometry didn't exist except as a vile, childish pun. Questions?

There were no questions. An hour later, "prigonometry" was all over the school, including the teachers' lounge. By the end of the month, it was the only thing anyone ever called Mr. Kirby's course, and Principal Milhouse had to tell him to stop putting students in detention for saying it.

Mr. Kirby had been in a bad mood ever since. On the day that what would happen happened, he was eating his solitary lunch in the teachers' lounge in an even worse mood. It was Friday, for one thing—the brink of a solitary, school-free, structureless weekend. Worse, it was Halloween.

In a bid to keep wild packs of teenagers off the streets, the school was hosting a Halloween dance that night. Students and staff had worked hard for weeks to promote it. Student Council painted and taped up banners in all the major hallways; Sunshine Society attached black and orange streamers and balloons to whatever didn't move; Mrs. Lewis in the principal's office led morning announcements with dance news for a week. Mr. Kirby was thoroughly bored by the whole pointless thing, but everyone else looked forward to it. That Halloween day, most students and many teachers had come to school in costume.

Mr. Kirby hated costume. He'd spent all morning trying to teach the properties of trapezoids to animals, cartoon characters, supernatural creatures, and what he thought might be prostitutes. Also, a student he didn't even know had dressed up as him. He'd passed the boy in the hallway before lunch and was about to commend him for neatness of dress when he noticed the writing on the boy's stick-on name tag: PRIGINOMETRY KIRBY.

(Misspelled.)

Mr. Kirby let it go—for the moment. It was his turn to serve as a chaperone at that night's dance, where he'd surely catch the boy doing something punishable. You could always catch a teenager doing *something* punishable.

The thought made him smile, which made Miss Westlake do a double-take as she passed his table. Hopefully, she smiled back. But her smile froze as he silently but clearly disapproved of her Wonder Woman costume.

Young lady, he thought, *you're an inappropriate role model.*

You big prig, she thought, *stick your slide rule where it hurts.*

BY EIGHT THAT evening, Mr. Kirby was half-deaf with noise, squinting through the dimness at the costumed figures gyrating all over the gym floor. He supposed that what they were doing was dancing and that what they were doing it to was music, but he disapproved all the same. Girls in his day had decent shame; boys in his time knew restraint.

Thin-lipped with censure, he checked the punchbowls for alcohol. The French teacher in charge of the refreshments table assured him that the punch was clean, but Mr. Kirby trusted no one in a French maid's costume, especially not a man with such hairy legs. He served himself a glass for inspection and took it back to the chaperones' row in the bleachers.

No one moved to make room for him, so he went up a couple of rows. He didn't notice until the stranger spoke that someone was already sitting there.

"I beg your pardon," Mr. Kirby said. "I'll move."

"I won't bite," said the stranger. "Have a seat."

Against his better judgment, Mr. Kirby did. It never occurred to him to offer the stranger his drink, but if it had, he would have reasoned that the man could see the refreshments table as well as he could.

It also never occurred to him that the stranger had said he *wouldn't* bite, not that he didn't.

Whoever he was, he was certainly strange enough. He had on a red-devil costume—the usual type, with pointy tail, plastic pitchfork, and satin horns on a headband—but his feet didn't look right; in the half-dark, they appeared to be bare, furry, and cloven. The facial hair was shaved in an odd pattern but appeared to be real. What bothered Mr. Kirby more were the eyes, which glowed like coals.

Out of nowhere, a memory flashed: a long-lost painting of his father's, a demonic face with tiny red lightbulbs cut through the canvas for eyes. The lights were attached to a battery taped to the back of the frame and could be switched on and off. Little Donovan stayed as far away from that piece as he possibly could, especially when the eyes were on. Buyers seemed to feel the same way about it; if he remembered right, it had never sold. What was the name of that painting, again? Had it ever had a name?

Had it really looked so much like this stranger?

He shivered—and then got a grip. That was then. This was now. He was at a high school Halloween dance in a badly lighted gym, and the colors in the stranger's eyes were reflections. What they reflected was none of his concern.

"WHAT DO YOU teach?" the man in the devil costume asked when the music dropped a few decibels.

"Geometry. The name's Kirby."

The stranger waited to be asked for his name in return but waited in vain.

"I *try* to teach them geometry," Mr. Kirby added, "but the darned kids are out of control. Can't teach them anything these days."

"Is that so?"

"A whole generation gone to hell in a handbasket. All they care about is themselves. They all want to be famous. They all think they're *artists*." The last word dripped with more contempt than he intended, but not much more. "Kids don't want to learn the skills to get a good steady job these days. They laugh at you for telling them real life is hard and education matters."

"Real life *is* hard," the stranger agreed, "and education *does* matter. What else is wrong?"

Mr. Kirby was on a roll, too angry to wonder why the stranger asked. He had a lifetime of stored-up resentments; he'd had a bad semester. It wasn't until he circled back to geometry several minutes later that the stranger spoke again.

"You're fond of Euclid?"

Mr. Kirby stopped to ponder. "I wouldn't say 'fond,' exactly, but he's the master. He understands reality." Another pause for thought. "I mean to say, he *understood*. He lived 2,300 years ago."

"Doesn't he still?"

"Pardon?"

"That is to say, don't his ideas live on? Aren't they immortal?"

"I don't think 'immortal' is the right word, but I suppose you could say his ideas will never die. That's true enough."

"They live on," the stranger agreed, "in the great marketplace of ideas. One grand geometry among all the others. Don't you think?"

"I do not," said Mr. Kirby, alarmed by the sideways turn of the conversation. "There's no geometry but Euclid's. It describes the world precisely and perfectly, and it works. It *has* worked for thousands of years."

"In this world, certainly. What about the others?"

"What others?"

The stranger laughed. "Come, now, Kirby, the world is various. The *worlds* are various. Do you think that 1 plus 1 always equals 2 or that a cone can't also be a polyhedron or that you live in a three-dimensional universe? Are you sure that your reality is real?"

By this time, Mr. Kirby was on his feet. "There's something in the punch, isn't there? Hoffman over there said there wasn't, but *you've* had something. I'd say you've had enough. Excuse me."

"Would you rather talk about prigonometry?" the stranger asked.

Shocked, Mr. Kirby turned. The man was leaning back on the bleachers now, completely at ease, smiling in a way he didn't like. There'd been no insult in the way he'd asked the question—it was only a question—but in a perfect world, his expression would have been against the law.

"We could talk about art instead, if you'd rather," the stranger said. "How about the Surrealists? Are you fond of Dalí? Or maybe you're an Abstract Expressionism man. Do you care for de Kooning? Klee, perhaps?"

"You leave art out of this," Mr. Kirby replied through clenched teeth. "I believe in reality. I believe in answers and logic and things that make sense and have a point. I don't believe in *you*." Why he'd said that last thing, he wasn't sure, but it felt true. "And while we're at it: Who are you?"

"Guess. Look in the details."

Unamused, Mr. Kirby glared at him for a long moment. "Damn you."

"No, damn *you*. I'll be shifting your paradigm now. Goodbye, Mr. Kirby."

The stranger made a swift, complicated gesture. A plane figure from non-Euclidean alternative geometry shimmered in midair, revolved in six dimensions, flashed all the colors of the infrared spectrum, turned itself outside up and downside in, and contrapositived Mr. Kirby.

THE ENTITY FORMERLY known as Don Kirby hated his new dimensions. He was parallel lines that met; he was special points at infinity; he was a curled-up string of spacetime intersecting random planes. He was light and color, symmetry and discord, the music of the spheres. To observers who knew the Earth, he was a Picasso, and he would inspire great works of art across the worlds forever.

SHORT FORM

THIS IS A true story.

Not my story, mind you, but his. He told it to me himself the last time I was in California. I've always found him to be a reliable source, and my brother and sister-in-law have corroborated some of the details, so I don't doubt his word.

Still, you don't know him, or me, or them, so you may want convincing. Fine—ask Mr. Boots yourself.

You should know straight up that the protagonist is a tabby cat. He owns my brother and sister-in-law in California, and he has a short-term lease on me whenever I visit. That's the nature of cats, of course. But Mr. Boots isn't just any cat. There's his size, for one thing; he could almost pass for a lineman for the 'Niners. There's also his temper. Several of the neighbors own show dogs, which are unacceptable to Mr. Boots, so he offs them.

The dogs, I mean. He may not off them technically—not really—but he does come home some nights with poodle fur in his claws, and I've actually seen him chase a Shih Tzu.

My brother and I are very proud of him. My sister-in-law says she forgives us for this.

But forgiveness has nothing to do with the story.

IT ALL STARTED when the Internal Revenue Service sent Mr. Boots a letter, demanding payment of unpaid taxes.

My brother laughed at first. "Idiots," he said. "Idiots with computers even more idiotic than they are. Which is *really* idiotic." My sister-in-law agreed but said he should call in the morning anyway to set things straight.

Mr. Boots went on washing his paws with unconcern. Later that evening, he mentioned the letter to some of the other neighborhood pets. (Excuse me—companion animals.) They all laughed too.

No one was laughing the next day, when the IRS refused to believe my brother, or a month later, when the IRS threatened to seize Mr. Boots' assets.

Well, OK, but Mr. Boots' total assets at the time were an L.L. Bean cat bed, several plastic food bowls, a blue china water dish, a ball with a bell inside, a yellow rubber squeaky bird, an assortment of catnip mice (used), and an earring that my sister-in-law thought she'd lost. The lot wouldn't fetch twenty bucks at a tax auction, but try telling that to a bureaucrat.

"He's a cat," my brother insisted over the phone. "He's named Mr. Boots, for Chrissakes. How many human beings would go around being named 'Mr. Boots'?"

There was a long silence before the revenue officer answered. "We aren't in the business of determining that."

My brother almost asked him what he *was* in the business of determining, not to mention how many times he'd had to repeat first grade, but he got a tentative grip at the last second. "I'm not kidding. He's a cat. He's furry. He coughs up hairballs. How many taxpayers cough up hairballs?"

"We aren't in the business of determining that either," the revenue officer said.

At that point, my brother handed the phone to my sister-in-law, who is a peace-loving woman with the patience of a saint. He said she started twitching after about thirty seconds and was still twitching the next morning.

The day my brother called to tell me his troubles, I had CNN on. While he went over the conversation with the revenue officer, citing chapter and verse, some weird-news segment came on, so I divided my attention.

Then my attention got totally undivided, and I told my brother to shut up for a second and turn on CNN.

You can look it up yourself if you don't believe me: There was a cat on TV, sitting at a table, eating people food off a people plate with a spoon. A few seconds later, the same cat was sitting at the same table eating Chinese food with chopsticks. I mean, the cat had *two chopsticks* in its right paw, and it was working them like a pro, shoveling food into its mouth without stopping for breath or dropping a single thing.*

"Damn," my brother marveled. "I can't do that."

"You're not so hot with a spoon either," I said.

Later, my brother would remember that Mr. Boots was in the room at the time. Neither of us thought anything of it until much later.

* CNN, July 2002, absolutely real.

THAT NIGHT, WHEN he made his social rounds, Mr. Boots discussed the TV clip with the other companion animals on the block. Bruno was skeptical; Binky was astonished; Bowser kept licking himself. As for Kitty Carlisle, she wasn't sure you could believe everything you saw on cable news, but she was willing to be convinced. If Mr. Boots could learn to do it himself, and show them . . .

Done, he said.

A few nights later, my brother and sister-in-law went out to dinner, and Mr. Boots let everyone in through the kitchen door, which he'd propped open with a dead mouse. He produced the silverware he'd hidden earlier in the day and calmly ate the mouse out of his favorite bowl with a fork and knife.

Everyone was impressed. Kitty Carlisle was so impressed that she spent the night.

MR. BOOTS' PERSONAL life is beside the point, as he'd be the first to tell you, but this sleepover is pertinent to what ultimately happened, because Kitty Carlisle gave him the idea.

Or so he says.

They woke the next morning to an argument in the kitchen. My brother and sister-in-law have a solid marriage, but the stress of the past few weeks was taking a toll. The IRS was always on the phone, in the mailbox, on their backs, and up their noses. They'd tried reason; they'd tried sarcasm; they'd offered notarized proof of Mr. Boots' felinity. Nothing had worked. The revenue officer on the case was hot for human blood, and he had it in his mind that Mr. Boots was a person pretending to be a cat.

Which made my brother and sister-in-law guilty of sheltering a tax fugitive, in his opinion, and he was determined to bring them to justice too, so now he was threatening them with an audit. The day before, my brother had lost patience and told the revenue officer to go to hell on a pogo stick. He'd forgotten to mention this conversation to his wife until breakfast.

Hence, the argument in the kitchen.

Mr. Boots and Kitty Carlisle listened with interest. It went on for a while, because both my brother and sister-in-law know a lot of words. Eventually, one of them left for work and slammed the door; the cats waited for the other one to leave for work and slam the door too. (I think my sister-in-law may have done it the second time, because Mr. Boots says all the pictures in the living room ended up crooked after.)

Kitty Carlisle thought for a long time. Then she said it was too bad that his people were having this trouble. She said it was also too bad that they couldn't torment the IRS back. That's what a cat would do, she said.

SOON AFTER THAT, the revenue officer stopped by in person to investigate. My brother and sister-in-law were both at work, but it was the cleaning lady's day, and she'd forgotten to pull the front door all the way shut when she left. She did that every so often.

Mr. Boots liked when that happened. He lost no time inviting the other companion animals over to watch TV. Maybe this time, they could figure out how to get one of those really dirty pay channels.

Binky and Bruno were fighting over the remote—Binky wanted *Gilligan's Island* reruns, and Bruno wanted MTV—when the doorbell rang. Instinctively, they all ran to hide in the kitchen.

All of them, that is, except Mr. Boots. It *was* his house. He sat in the middle of the living room, watching the front door to see what would happen, and when the revenue officer let himself in, Mr. Boots didn't object.

"I'll be damned," the man said. "They *do* have a cat. I bet it doesn't have papers. What's your name, girl?"

Girl?

The man jumped up on the coffee table before Mr. Boots got his fangs all the way through his ankle and tried to hold the animal at bay with his briefcase. "Down, girl! Down! I'm a federal officer!"

Mr. Boots was unimpressed. He started to climb up on the coffee table.

"I'm the law!" the man insisted. "I'm with the Treasury Department! I've got ID! Wait—I'll show you!"

Fine, if it would humor him. Mr. Boots waited while the man fished out the card, wondering how long it would take him to realize that he was showing ID to a cat.

"I'm on official government business," the man said. "See? I'm with the IRS."

In the kitchen, they heard the "IRS" part. Kitty Carlisle hissed. Binky howled. Bowser licked himself harder.

And on the coffee table in the living room . . .

Well.

AN HOUR LATER, Mr. Boots was seated comfortably at the head of the dining-room table, a linen napkin tucked into his collar and a fork and knife in his paws. The smell of cooking was getting delicious.

Kitty Carlisle poked her head around the corner. "He's ready."

"Excellent," Mr. Boots said. "Now bring me the short form."

WHEN MR. BOOTS finished recounting these events, he asked whether I believed him.

"No," I said. "You've been smoking catnip again, haven't you?"

He gave me one of those Cheshire smiles and started washing his face.

Later, though, I found a plastic pocket protector half-buried in the garden, and my sister-in-law mentioned that she couldn't find the big cleaver. Coincidences? Maybe.

But it's a matter of record that the IRS never bothered Mr. Boots again.

SK8 PARK

FINALLY, THE TOWNSPEOPLE had had it up to here, so the mayor, the police chief, and the school principals called a town meeting at the high school gym.

As the townspeople filed in, most of them shook their heads over the once-pristine basketball court, now scarred, broken, and seamed with skid marks left by their nemeses. Special taxes were being levied to pay for the repairs before basketball season; otherwise, the Springfield Owls would have to play their home games at the YMCA. There was a great deal of talk about horsewhippings and military school.

The Town of Springfield had tried everything within reason. When the teenagers started skateboarding downtown, the city offered them the high school gym instead. When they ruined the basketball court, the city offered them the old, unused tennis courts in Westside Park. But the courts were too broken and bumpy for the kids; the kids were too loud and destructive for the neighbors. Also, they left trash everywhere: used gum, cigarette butts, beer cans, and worse. After that, the town dug into its recreation fund to buy skateboard ramps for Eastside Park, as well as lots of brightly painted trash barrels. The kids destroyed everything in less than a week—all but the trash barrels, which stayed as pristine as the day they were purchased.

None of these good-faith efforts mattered, though. The youngsters had never wanted a skateboard park in the first place; they wanted to skateboard downtown. So skateboarding downtown was what they did. Day after day, night after night, they terrorized elderly pedestrians, small dogs, and absent-minded citizens by whizzing around corners unannounced. They did damaging tricks off the town's expensive brick-and-concrete planters. They defaced the town's expensive brick pavers with skid marks, used gum, cigarette butts, spilled beer, and worse.

Somehow, the police never managed to catch them, but the downtown merchants saw a lot of them. Whenever school was out, skating was in.

The meeting at the gym that night was to vote on the two options left to town officials: outlawing skateboarding or outlawing teenagers. Popular sentiment favored outlawing both.

Mayor Goodman listened patiently to speakers on both sides of the issue before calling for a vote. Before he could call it, however, a man he'd never seen before stood up and asked for the floor. He'd take only a minute, he said. On his way to the microphone, he handed business cards to the mayor, the police chief, and the principals. Mayor Goodman introduced him straight from the card: H. Grimm, consultant with Piper Planners.

Mr. Grimm spoke for well over a minute. His proposal was well received, and when it was put to a vote, it carried unanimously.

SPRINGFIELD SKATEBOARD PARK, donated by the Piper Foundation, opened in June. Every skateboarder in town who agreed to use it would get a year of free pizzas, also paid for by the foundation. Mr. Grimm had suggested holding the opening ceremony after curfew because after curfew was the youngsters' favorite time to skate.

Every skateboarder in town showed up. So did most of the townspeople. So did old Mr. Youngblood, who had his Army service revolver loaded and carefully tucked into the waistband of his trousers; he'd been terrorized one too many times by skateboarders in the past year and was prepared to administer justice if terror occurred tonight.

Mr. Grimm spoke, briefly. He praised the town for being so supportive of its young people. He praised the foundation for being so generous. He hoped that this solution would satisfy demand. At last, he flipped the switch that turned on the floodlights.

The townspeople blinked in the megawatt glare and then blinked at the park itself, which was supposed to be a replica of Springfield's downtown. But where the brick pavers should have been was ice; where the warm night air should have been was fog. It was hard to make out the replica brick-and-concrete planters, but the recycled trash barrels (still as pristine as the day they were purchased) were orange enough to be faintly visible.

Mr. Grimm unlocked the gate in the chain-link fence and pulled it open. "Go on," he told the nearest skateboarder.

The boy scowled, shrugged, spat. "That's *ice*, man."

"It's not," Mr. Grimm assured him. "It's a special effect. We want this to look good, don't we? Go on."

Unreassured but unwilling to look scared, the boy spat again and then walked through the gate. The fog swallowed him.

"Go on," Mr. Grimm told the next in line.

One by one, the young people went through the gate and were swallowed by the fog. It was a curious thing: The park got quieter the more of them went in.

When all the skateboarders had passed through, the consultant closed and locked the gate.

"Hey, my boy's in there!" one parent protested. "How's he getting out?"

Mr. Grimm asked him who'd said anything about getting out.

THE CHIEF OF police wanted to arrest Mr. Grimm for abduction, but in the end, there were no grounds. There was only the contract. The townspeople had wanted freedom from the town's trashy, mouthy skateboarders, and the consulting firm had delivered.

"Can't you bring them back?" one mother demanded.

Of course he could, Mr. Grimm said, but the townspeople couldn't afford it. They'd already sold their souls to get rid of the skateboarders in the first place.

They *could* do one thing, he said: wait. The kids would come back in a few years, no longer kids. The townspeople might not like what they came back as, but that wouldn't be Piper's problem. When you hire consultants, you pays your money and takes your choice.

HACIENDA

NO ONE KNEW where the house had come from. It had simply appeared in the New Mexico back country on a day when a needy family needed shelter most. The Garcias had lost their rental home that morning after weeks of pleading. Carlos lost his job when the work went overseas, and weeks of searching for a new one hadn't panned out. Juanita's earnings from taking in bookkeeping were too little even to keep the water bill paid. In a much shorter time than he would have given Anglos, the landlord evicted them. The family were on foot that day, taking everything they could carry in their battered, mismatched suitcases, walking along the edge of the road from nothing, perhaps going toward nothing, but moving. Juanita had cousins in Las Cruces, a few miles away; if they could reach them, perhaps they'd know where her family could turn.

Maria saw the house first. At first, her mother scolded her for telling tales. There were no houses around, only scrub and brush, rocks and sand in all directions.

But the closer they got, the clearer the outlines of the house grew. It was small, adobe, humble, inviting, with blue-washed wooden doors and shutters, with clay pots on the front porch and strings of peppers drying on pegs by the front door. The house seemed to smile at them, at the weary family with so little left to smile back about.

Then José noticed something and ran to see. "Mama! Papa!" he cried.

His father chased the boy down but stopped short when he saw too: The tiled plaque by the front door read THE GARCIAS. Next to the house was Carlos's abandoned, broken-down Ford pickup truck, nearly the same shade of turquoise as the letters on the tiled plaque. The key was in the ignition. The family had had to leave the truck behind at the rental house; there'd been no money to repair it, but the owner of the rental house had taken it in partial payment all the same.

Cautiously, Juanita held the children with her on the road while Carlos climbed into the truck cab. The key (*his* key) turned smoothly; the engine started. It ran as though nothing was wrong and never had been.

"I don't understand, Carlito," his wife said.

"Neither do I," he admitted. "But we should wait to ask whoever lives here."

The family looked around the property while they waited, and every new discovery was a wonderful surprise. There were the children's own toys scattered around the yard, magically transported to this place. When they looked in the windows, they saw all the belongings they'd had to leave behind, there inside the house in familiar arrangements. Even Juanita's beloved flowerbeds were present, fully intact.

The front door was unlocked. Eventually, they succumbed to temptation and entered. Everything was as they remembered except that the larder was full, and so was the refrigerator.

The family had a tiny snack (they set aside a few coins to pay for it) while they waited for the owners of the home to return. Night fell. No one returned.

"I guess we could stay here tonight," Carlos said. "If the owners come home, we'll explain. We'll be no worse off if they throw us out."

Juanita went to the back bedroom so he and the children wouldn't see her tears.

THE HOMEOWNERS NEVER came home—not the next day, not the next week, not two months down the road. The house seemed to grow more theirs every day, with little forgotten touches of their old home emerging now and then. José found the baseball he'd lost, and also the skateboard. Maria's favorite yellow dress was in a box of children's clothes that appeared on the porch; the berry stains that had spoiled it were gone. A framed photo of Juanita's favorite aunt—the one she was named for—materialized on a table in the living room, even though they'd sold the silver frame for grocery money months ago. Even Carlos recovered his pocket watch, which his grandfather had left him and which had fallen through a hole in his pocket; it turned up in the refrigerator, nicely chilled but still ticking.

What was more, the house had been lucky for all of them. Carlos found a new job in Las Cruces, a better job than the old one. A neighbor (how had they not noticed the other houses before?) helped Juanita find part-time bookkeeping work. The children liked their new school and made new friends.

Of course the Garcias asked questions. They asked everyone from the mayor's help line to their state representative's office. But no one could answer. As far as the county clerk's records were concerned, the house had always been there, had always been theirs, belonged to them free and clear, and those were certainly Carlos's and Juanita's signatures on the deed. Not even the relatives in Las Cruces believed the story. The Garcias had *always* lived near the Mendozas, Juanita's cousin said, and she should stop telling these silly stories about magical houses. Now, would the Garcias like to come to the Mendozas for Cinco this year, or would they like to host their cousins?

The family thanked the Virgin and the Son at Mass every Sunday in the nearby village. They were grateful for their good fortune, and they helped others who needed a little good fortune because they knew so well what it was like to be unlucky.

Fortune is a wheel, however, and sometimes the wheel is crooked.

IN DECEMBER, WHEN Congress let out for the holidays, the politicians went back to their home states to troll for funds, publicity, and trouble. Sen. August Trumbull (R-Georgia) was in desperate need of all three. He wanted to be president, and he needed a platform. By then, of course, just wanting to be president was a good enough reason to run, but it would help to have an Issue. It should be something big, something controversial, something that would keep him on the front pages and at the tops of newscasts while he Prayerfully Considered His Duty to His Country. He preferred that the something not involve fracking, which his biggest donors were pressuring him to push.

On the way out of his office, he bumped into Mike.

Sen. Miguel Flores (D-New Mexico) had problems of his own. He had to crack down on immigration because his corporate masters wanted it, which was fine with him to a point, but now they wanted all undocumented immigrants shot. That would play poorly with 57 percent of the voters back home, and he wanted to be president.

The senators knew each other's troubles. They eyed each other shrewdly while they chatted about nothing special, waiting for the elevator. Trumbull was the one who suggested drinks.

After the drinks, they parted with a deal, which was this: Senator Trumbull would press for shootings while Senator Flores did battle for fracking. Each

man would take the other's heat while advancing the other's agenda, and in
the spring, they'd both announce for president. Each man thought the other
would really be running for veep.

SENATOR FLORES FOUND the staff of his Albuquerque office bored
and restive. Not much had happened since his last visit home; there'd been
a few crackpot stories in the news, but that was all.

"What stories?" he asked.

His New Mexico press director flicked through the files on his tablet.
There was one crazy report the boss might like, referred to them by a state
representative's office. Apparently, a house had just *appeared* one day to a
Hispanic family near Las Cruces, and the man of the family was trying to
find out who owned it so he could pay for it properly.

Ah, there it was. "Peyote, I bet," the deputy press director said, handing
the tablet over.

Senator Flores read the notes. He read them again, and he smiled. He
told his girl to get Senator Trumbull's office on the phone.

ALL THE HEADLINES that week were Second Coming screamers: *Hot
Hacienda! Undocumented House! Mystery Migrant Mansion!*

Senator Trumbull read them with pleasure as the campaign van drove
him back to the house for another press conference. It had been so very,
very easy, and such fun too. The Garcias might not be undocumented
themselves—there were the pesky matters of Carlos's green card and Juanita's
naturalization certificate—but you couldn't prove anything about the house.
It looked foreign; it had clearly crossed borders. Any papers it had were
probably forged.

The house itself wasn't talking. It stood there silently, humbly, quietly,
protecting the family inside from the press as best it could.

Juanita's cousins were there for moral support. They'd brought the strings
of drying peppers inside, secured the clay pots, closed the blue-washed
shutters. By now, everyone knew the drill. The politicians would gather at
the edge of the front yard, blocking the road, while the local police formed
a line between them and the house. The officials talked talked talked while
scruffy people shouted questions and cameras rolled. It would last about an
hour, from setup to teardown, and then everyone would go away.

As soon as the mob left today, the cousins inside the house would go out to finish their holiday shopping. Christmas was days away.

On this day, though, Senator Trumbull had a fine lump of coal to drop in the Garcia family's stockings. That was the purpose of the press conference. He was announcing it early, to give the media time to gin up public outrage. All publicity was good publicity for a president-in-waiting.

He was just finishing the *New York Wanker* story when he remembered the phone call from Flores the day before. A small frown creased his satisfied face. Flores didn't like this new tack. He said you couldn't evict a family for no good reason—not a poor family with small children, not on live TV, absolutely not on Christmas Eve.

"We're not evicting the *family*, Mike," he'd said patiently. "We're evicting the *house*. We can't shoot it with them in it. We're just giving them fair warning before—"

"Who is this 'we'? This is *your* doing, Gus, not mine. You're going to wreck the deal."

Trumbull uttered a few easy vulgarities and hung up. The deal was already wrecked as far as he was concerned. Flores wasn't enthusiastic about the pro-fracking bill that Trumbull's backers wanted, and he himself was already bored with border politics. Why not have some fun and grab some headlines before calling it quits?

"It's Senator Flores again, sir," an aide told him, handing over the other phone.

The text read, "Also, a little house isn't a hacienda, you fucking dummy."

Trumbull shrugged and deleted it.

CHRISTMAS EVE AFTERNOON was cold, overcast, and threatening snow, which pleased Senator Trumbull. The eviction would be more photogenic that way.

Inside the small house, the Garcia and Mendoza families readied themselves for the worst. They had a Legal Aid lawyer and a social worker from José's school inside with them, which made the place snug, but at least everyone had a place to sit if they sat on luggage. The family's battered suitcases were packed again; several large cardboard boxes were taped up ready; everything would fit in the bed of Carlos's truck. The children would ride to the Mendozas' with their cousins, and the church had donated a few sleeping bags for the family to use.

Juanita wept. She didn't want to leave, of course, but she mostly didn't want her loved ones humiliated on coast-to-coast television for some political stunt. Maria, too young to know humiliation from gumdrops, gave Mama a hug and told her not to cry because Santa was coming.

The knock came promptly at noon. The sheriff had the eviction papers and formally served them; many officers escorted the family from the house (and helped them load the old Ford pickup); no one paid any attention to the protests of the lawyer, the social worker, or the large silent crowd that had come to bear witness. An aide to the senator made a point of opening the shutters because (he said) transparency.

When everything was done, Senator Trumbull strode to the front door and posed there. He smiled winningly. He shook hands with the National Guardsmen and patted their large automatic weapons (they'd be executing the house shortly) while cameras clicked and rolled. There were a few boos from the back of the crowd, but soft ones. No one wanted to cross the Powers on a holy day.

"I'll take one last look around inside," he told an aide. "In case some of them are hiding. Keep the goddamn reporters out."

No one knew who closed the blue-washed front door behind him or how the blue-washed shutters came to be shut again.

The flash of heat and light surprised everyone. Those standing nearest the house stepped back—faster as the heat intensified. The small adobe house grew hotter yet, hotter still, hot as an oven.

The Garcias and Mendozas stopped their vehicles in the road and jumped out, intending to go back to help, but it was too late. Even that far away, the odor of roast pork was strong. The smell was changing to something else when the house collapsed in a heap of adobe ash.

"Mama, look!" José said, tugging on his mother's sleeve with one hand and pointing upward with the other. Fat, clean snowflakes were falling.

IT SNOWED THE rest of Christmas Eve and well into Christmas Day. The Garcias and Mendozas celebrated at church and at the homes of their well-wishers. As a Christmas gift, the community would be building a new house for the Garcias, anything they wanted. They wanted one just like the humble adobe house where they'd been so happy. They would help with the building themselves.

Senator Flores presided over the groundbreaking, turning the earth with a silver spade with a red satin bow tied to the handle. Tomorrow was Three Kings' Day, Día de Los Reyes, but everyone wanted to get an early start. (Also, Flores wanted the photo op.)

A few miles away, what was left of the adobe house smoldered in peace, watched over by Guardsmen and curious locals. No one could stand to watch for long, however. The snow had masked the ruins somewhat, but the heat of the ash had melted the snow, and now the foul stench of dirty burning fur was stronger than ever. No one knew then that the smell would linger for years.

DEAD PEASANTS

THE DAY MISS Martingale died was the day Fountainhead HealthMed Insurers had been waiting for. Dead Peasant #1,000,000 was a great achievement, a glowing testament to the vision of FHMI Chairman Flyster, who'd said all along that there was greater profit in killing off the customers.

Miss Martingale hadn't been much of a customer, but that was the whole point. Only just too wealthy for Medicaid, only just too young for Medicare, too poor to pay full price and ineligible for government subsidies, she'd struggled to pay the premiums on her tiny policy, which FHMI kept threatening to cancel. She couldn't afford to use the insurance because the deductible climbed every time she did, but everyone said she needed it because of her weak heart. Accordingly, she sacrificed to keep her coverage, going without food, heat, running water, and even medicines many weeks, especially when her nephews were late in helping with the bills. She was a nobody, a nothing, a cipher whose pitiful, hard-paid premiums wouldn't pay Flyster's lunch tab.

But now that she was dead, she was the whole reason FHMI was still in business. She was a Dead Peasant. She'd been easy to cheat, fun to bewilder, a joy to make cry on the phone, and now (along with 999,999 other corpses) she was the corporation's main revenue stream.

To celebrate his millionth Dead Peasant, Chairman Flyster ordered big pay bumps for top management and FHMI bumper stickers for all employees in good standing. He purchased a $3,000 shower curtain for the executive bathroom on *Flyster One* and hired a more attractive flight crew. He bought a small Caribbean island. He granted interviews to the top business telejournalists, thanking God for his good fortune in being able to help so many deserving people, who were the first thing he thought about in the morning and the last thing he thought about at night.

"Bullshit, Frank," the president of his Fountainhead American subsidiary warned him privately. "Dial it back."

Flyster fired the president, installed his son-in-law in the job, and bought a new yacht to park at the new island. To defray the costs, he raised rates on the company's cheapest policies by 20 percent and rolled back coverage.

"It doesn't look good, Mr. Flyster," the head of Managed Expectations told him. "Not every business journalist is too dumb to connect the dots."

Flyster fired her too. Most business journalists were exactly that dumb, and thoroughly paid for, so employing someone to manage their expectations was a waste of good money. He gave the job to a recently discarded mistress and paid her in jewelry instead of cash. He spent the difference on hair plugs.

He'd been brilliant—a master of good old-fashioned American cutthroat capitalism—and he deserved these perks. Everyone said so.

Who knew, or cared, what he'd done with the premiums?

His plan had been simple: Secretly take out life insurance on the poorest, most vulnerable customers; frustrate, upset, and frighten them to suicide; and collect the death benefits. Anyone could have thought of it, but he was the one who had, so he deserved the rewards.

Taking out the secret insurance had been easy. After all, nobody read the fine print in policies. Frustrating, upsetting, and frightening the policyholders had been easy too. He outsourced the corporation's customer service to an offshore vendor with a bad reputation and installed a complicated phone tree that hung up on callers randomly or transferred them to completely different companies, also at random. He canceled more insurance through a fun computer game that all employees were urged to play: Win a game, and the computer wiped out a policy *and* paid you $1. Most employees earned most of their income through the game.

The next phase was a snap too. Flyster had the procedures manuals updated, replacing the scripts and step lists with ultracomplicated decision trees that led nowhere, infuriating callers and call-center personnel alike. Better yet, he decreed that the company would no longer keep records of individual customer-service calls; they were randomized at the end of every business day. The extra layers of complication ensured that no problem could ever be solved. Enraged by these impediments, most customers stopped calling, which meant that fewer call-center personnel were needed, which meant that Flyster could convert the savings into a beach house for his other mistress.

He decided to build it on the tiny plot of land that had been the last of Miss Martingale's inheritance—the one she'd had to mortgage, remortgage, and then sell to FHMI at a loss to pay her ever-rising health insurance premiums. It was a fitting site for a beach house for the other mistress of a good old-fashioned American cutthroat capitalist.

Her nephews honored Miss Martingale's last request by scattering her ashes over the plot at dawn a month after the funeral. It was coincidence that the contractor broke ground for the beach house later the same morning, with Chairman Flyster, the other mistress, and her three Akitas in attendance.

Flyster, offended that the contractor still wouldn't work for minimum wage, relieved his feelings by spitting. To add insult to mortal injury, he spat on a bit of what had been Miss Martingale.

LATE THAT NIGHT, Flyster, the other mistress, and the three Akitas slept soundly in the Magnolia Suite of Big Pink Hotel, tuckered out from spending death benefits in town. The mistress was still wearing the gaudy baguette-cut bracelet that Flyster had tossed on her pillow before lights out.

The lights weren't out long, however. In the half-hour after midnight, a blue orb materialized in the living room, glowing faintly. It bounced around for a few seconds, seemingly uncertain what to do, until another orb appeared. Then another. And another.

In the master bedroom, one of the dogs whined in its sleep.

The orbs waited. When it was clear that nothing else was going to happen, one of them blinked out for a few seconds, returning with a host of others.

Slowly, steadily, the living room of the Magnolia Suite filled with faintly glowing blue orbs—thousands and then tens of thousands. When their numbers exceeded the room's capacity, the windows began to buckle and crack.

Half-awakened by the buckling and cracking, the mistress mumbled a name. Not Flyster's.

Still more orbs arrived, squeezing under doors, around windows, and through vents. By now, the faint blue glow was a collective blue blaze, bright as midday, and as the first orbs popped into the master bedroom, the Akitas started to bark.

Flyster sat bolt upright in bed, his toupee keeling to starboard. The other mistress shot under the covers.

"What's the meaning of this?" the chairman demanded. "How did you get in here?"

No one answered. Perturbed, he lunged for his glasses on the night table and jammed them on.

"Who are you?"

No sooner did he ask than some of the orbs began changing form. Here a face, there a shoulder, hair and elbows and hips appeared as the orbs took human shape and slowly advanced on the bed.

"*What* are you?" Flyster demanded.

The first entity to reach him was the one that had been Miss Martingale. She'd used a gas oven and was slightly blue yet, but determined. Her pale eyes, so mild and bewildered in life, blazed with newfound ferocity.

The entity floating next to her cut Flyster's throat with the straight razor he'd used to slit his own wrists. While the other mistress screamed and screamed and the dogs barked and barked (but no one outside the suite heard a sound), Miss Martingale dipped a bony fingertip into the blood to paint a dollar sign on the dead man's forehead.

Eventually, the other mistress fainted, and the Dead Peasants cleaned up most of the mess that was left of Flyster. They peeled him for fun but let the dogs eat him.

FUNNY MONEY

DANTE MIGHT HAVE put ToiletAir on one of the deep circles of Hell had there been air travel in his day. That wasn't the airline's name, of course—only what travelers called it behind its back. A toilet was as aerodynamic and comfortable as one of its flights, with equal amenities and competitively friendly service.

Jayson Grayson flew ToiletAir on business, which acquainted him with hardship. Even the airline's private lounges were tainted by the public hell of its planes. Like most regulars, Jayson drank before boarding.

It was a cold night in November the first time he thought he'd had too much. The man sitting next to him at the bar—middle-aged, nondescript, might have been anything from an orthodontist to a state senator—scribbled something on a piece of greenish paper and slid it over to him.

The paper was a $50 bill. The man had drawn a cartoon speech bubble coming out of Ulysses S. Grant's mouth and written these words inside the bubble: *Hey baby, how about it?*

"Not even for a Benjamin," Jayson said. "And never the fuck with you."

The man shrugged, took the bill back, and ordered another drink.

It wasn't that Jayson was truly offended. Still, he didn't care for stereotypes, and a quickie at the airport was one for a reason. Moreover, the come-on lacked a certain panache. Jayson was a man of worldly, refined taste; you couldn't tempt him in London or Jakarta or Omaha with a wax apple. Neither could bad punctuation win his heart.

There was this, too: The man was paunchy and plain. Jayson liked money, but not *that* much.

His flight that evening was uneventful. By the time he checked in at the hotel, he'd forgotten about the proposition in the airport lounge.

He'd also forgotten about going to the bank before leaving home, so he stopped by the branch in the lobby with his platinum card. "Hundreds, please," he told the pretty teller, who smiled at him hopefully as she counted them out.

The sales meeting went well. Lunch with the clients went even better. When the check came, Jayson took one of the hundreds out of his billfold and was folding the waiter wallet over it when something on the money caught his eye.

In bright-blue ink (the color the man at the airport had used), someone had drawn a speech bubble for Benjamin Franklin and written these words inside it: *Hey, baby, how about it?*

Jayson noted the correct punctuation and chose to ignore the rest. Smiling (but it was a strained smile), he snapped the waiter wallet shut before the client could see.

IT HAPPENED AGAIN the next day, back home and after a good night's sleep. The sales team went out for drinks after work to celebrate Jayson's close, and he'd offered to pick up the last round himself, which would mean using one of the hundreds. At the last instant, he remembered and excused himself.

In the men's room, he held a bill up to the light. Benjamin Franklin winked at him—actually winked. Not a hallucination; not the second mojito. Then, as he watched, a bright-blue cartoon bubble drew itself on the paper, and tiny writing appeared inside it:

Not even for a me?

Jayson decided to stop drinking for a few days. He tore the bill into tiny pieces, flushed the pieces, and paid the tab with plastic instead.

IT WAS NO good. Thereafter, whatever Jayson did, $100 bills followed him around. He got change for them at the bank; he used cards instead of cash; he wrote checks; he deliberately carried nothing larger than a five. Yet his wallet was still full of hundreds at the end of every day, and no matter which one he took out, Benjamin Franklin winked at him from it. Jayson tore up the bills, but the Founding Flirt only reappeared on new ones.

This was odd too: Franklin was starting to look good. Whether it was a trick of whatever light Jayson was standing in at the time or a function of familiarity, the portrait on the bill got more attractive each time. The balding, jowly elder of the familiar Duplessis portrait seemed to be youthening, and there was a distinct twinkle in the eyes—particularly the right one. Jayson had started looking at it first. The right eye was friendlier; also, it was the one that winked.

As for the messages, there'd been more. Most were silly lines, well known to experienced daters. But that twinkle in the eyes took the curse off *If I say you have a great body, will you hold it against me?* and *Is this love at first sight, or should I come back?* The eyes were blue now, blue as clear Caribbean waters, blue as Blue Curaçao, blue as star-cut sapphires and—

Well, they were blue. The rest of the portrait stayed resolutely greenish.

By now, Jayson knew he was mad. He swore off drinking again.

But people at work were noticing. He was looking older, heavier, and grayer lately, with a colorless complexion and a dull eye, all of which was no good for business. "You're going to scare the clients, Jay-Jay," the boss said. "Take a couple of hours off. Get some rest."

THE NIGHT THAT led to everything else was the night Ben turned colors.

Jayson's day had been a long, annoying one. There'd been petty troubles of all kinds at the office—political squabbles, client complaints, PowerPoint presentations—and things hadn't gone well after work either. All the good ellipticals at the gym were taken; the steam room smelled of old guys; some jerk dinged his Audi in the parking lot. Even the stop at the liquor store was bad. The cute clerk who sometimes flirted with him wasn't on duty that night, and the hatchet-faced Goth at the cash register sneered at his purchase.

Jayson returned the sneer with interest. People drank rum year-round, so what was wrong with Blue Curaçao in November?

To intimidate the mean boy, he started to pay with a hundred—and took it back when he saw what it looked like.

The portrait was still in color when he got it home, behind locked doors. It had also changed clothes. Instead of the fusty Colonial costume, the man still identified on the bill as Franklin was wearing a Hawaiian shirt, mostly open. His long blond hair blew gently in a very local wind. His blue eyes twinkled in his warmly tanned face, which appeared to be late twenties at most, early thirties at worst.

He might have been Jayson himself a couple of years ago, that summer at Riviera Maya.

Jayson turned on all the floodlights in his kitchen and studied the bill again. "Impossible," he told it firmly.

The bright-blue cartoon bubble drew itself while he watched, with these words inside: *Says who?*

He'd never talked to money before. Doing so had never occurred to him. But if he could talk to it, and it could talk back . . .

"Are you real?"

The bubble expanded, and new words appeared: *Come here and find out.*

Jayson wasn't sure that he should. But the right eye was twinkling blue fire at him, and the shirt (Tommy Bahama?) was invitingly open. He held the bill a foot from his face.

Closer, Jay-Jay, the speech bubble said.

All right, then, he thought; in for a penny, in for a pound. He pressed the bill to his lips.

The bill kissed back. Shocked, he dropped it—and watched the message in the speech bubble change:

Real enough for you?

Jayson left the hundred lying on the floor; he opened the new bottle and drank directly from it. Half the bottle later, he looked in the nearest mirror. His reflection was greenish.

BY THE END of the month, not even Jayson's closest friends could rationalize away the change. He'd become secretive, reclusive, antisocial, spending all his free time at home with the blinds drawn and the phones off. Paradoxically, he also seemed more relaxed and happier than they'd seen him for quite a while.

"He's seeing someone new," Clayton said at the fourth party Jayson turned down.

Victor reminded him that Jayson had never turned down a chance to flaunt a new man at a party before. He was vicious that way.

Darius thought downers. Erich thought painkillers and white wine. Lane said they were all crazy; Jayson was getting old and giving in to pizza and pay-TV porn.

They agreed that this would explain it. No one gave it another thought.

JAYSON HAD TO fire the maid when he overslept and she caught him in bed with Ben. She didn't see anything really—only a man with a $100 bill on the pillow next to him—but it was hard to explain what she *did* see. It was easier to fire her.

He hoped that his boss wasn't starting to feel the same way. He'd missed some work lately, and at least one client had complained about his appearance, not to mention his clothes. Pirate shirts were a bridge too far in business.

In truth, they weren't pirate shirts, but Jayson chose not to explain.

"I wish we could get married," he told Ben one evening while he dined (on take-out) by candlelight. "But marriage is a piece of paper, isn't it?"

I'm a piece of paper, Ben wrote back.

"Don't make jokes. Same-sex marriage is legal now." He smiled sourly. "But I guess it wouldn't cover this."

Then cover this, baby.

Jayson did, and finished his dinner later.

THE BIG MEETING with the big prospective client in Boston was set for the following week. Jayson was the ace closer, the one you sent to sign valuable prospects, so he was the one the boss sent. But first, the boss had a come-to-Jesus with him about first impressions, ordering him to get a haircut and wear a man's shirt.

As usual, his airline ticket was on ToiletAir.

Jayson had a couple of margaritas in the airline lounge the afternoon of departure. He ate most of the snack platter and a couple of bags of airline pretzels. Then he ordered a new snack platter for himself, along with peanuts and a Tequila Sunrise. By that time, the other patrons of the lounge were avoiding him, partly because of the frilly Colonial shirt, partly because of the gluttony, but mostly because he kept talking—and laughing—to himself.

Mile High Club, Ben wrote.

"No airplane bathrooms," Jayson said.

Airport, not airplane.

"No airport bathrooms either. They're filthy."

What Ben wrote next was filthier, but it made Jayson laugh. A municipal judge who'd been giving him the eye gave up and left the bar.

On board the flight, the woman sitting next to him asked to change seats as soon as the seat-belt light went out. The flight attendant took one look at Jayson—who was drunkenly, obscenely kissing a $100 bill that he'd flattened against the window—and moved the woman to her own seat in the back.

The man in the aisle seat ignored him. He was a frequent flyer and knew to ignore things.

Enough flirting, Ben wrote. *Want to consummate this?*

Drunk as he was, Jayson still had an intact sense of irony. He laughed in Ben's pretty face. "If this is 'flirting,' honey, consummation would kill me."

Want to find out?

The question took Jayson aback enough to clear some of the fog from his brain. It suddenly occurred to him that he was in public and that people could see, hear, and speculate. Carefully, he folded down his seat-back tray and set Ben on it.

"How?" he whispered.

The speech bubble expanded, and the familiar bright-blue handwriting said *Write your name*.

Jayson switched on his overhead light to study his money. The portrait was the same: a blue-eyed hunk in an open Hawaiian shirt, long hair blowing attractively, enigmatic smile dimpling. He could almost smell Ben's cologne (Aramis?), feel the warm sea breezes, hear the steel drums on the beach.

Ben's right eye twinkled brilliantly as it winked. His sculpted pecs rippled in the overhead light.

Hey, baby, how about it?

"Oh, hell, why not," Jayson said aloud.

He had a fountain pen in an inside coat pocket. As he bent over the bill, Ben's speech bubble disappeared, and a neon arrow said SIGN HERE. Jayson did.

The instant he made the last stroke of his signature, everything on the bill disappeared, leaving the paper blank. Then six-point text started scrolling up the blank: the text of the contract Jayson had just signed. It went on and on and on.

While Jayson watched in horror, the text scrolled faster. He felt himself grow dizzy, then faint, and the last thing he knew was the sensation of being sucked into two dimensions.

THE BLUE-EYED HUNK in the window seat pocketed the bill before its new occupant could protest. When the cute flight attendant came by, he winked at her. An hour later, he joined the Mile High Club with her, after which he spent Jayson on airline Scotch, proving once again that a fool and his money are soon parted.

In the till in the stewards' galley, Jayson burned in impotent fury. His speech bubble expanded and contracted violently, but no one saw. At the end of the flight, the attendant who closed out the till accidentally dropped him, and later, the cleaning crew accidentally swept him under a gap in the carpet. Jayson flew ToiletAir—coach class—for the rest of his life.

LORD LUCRE'S TALE
[A FABLE]

ONCE THERE WERE, and were not, a handsome rich nobleman with a beautiful rich noblewife and two charming rich noblechildren. The Earl and Countess of Lucre, the Lady Gimme, and the Viscount of Graft lived in Unitranche Castle, on a large, stately estate where the sun always shone and the peasants always whistled while they worked. Indeed, Lord and Lady Lucre could have whistled themselves if they'd wanted—they had much to whistle about—but they didn't care to work. Nor did they have to. Their titles entitled the Lucres to the best fruits of other people's labor, which included their most musical whistling.

NOW, ONE DAY, Lady Gimme had to have her tutor slaughtered. The tutor had caused her to read (*so* tedious), and in the course of it, he showed her a heretical book—that is to say, a book not bound in golden plates studded with precious gems, a book not embellished with costly enamels of state-approved saints. Inside was worse yet. The pages were of coarse stuff, not fine vellum, not lavishly illuminated by starving artisans working by rushlight in freezing garrets. The text did not praise *Dieu et mon droit, jus primae noctis*, or absolute right of demesne. It failed to demonstrate the will of God in M'Lord's unalienable right to corvée.

(*Corvée*, of course, means labor provided by villeins to the lord of the manor. They spoke a lot of French and Latin in Unitranche Castle because they could.)

This book cannot be named. Lady Gimme ordered it properly bound and appropriately jeweled before she would touch it and then touched it only long enough to be affronted by the middling quality of the emeralds. She had the stones stripped off and sold for mad money without bothering to open the book, let alone note what it was called. For daring to expose Lady Gimme to mediocre goods, the tutor was thrown into the White Dungeon of the Black Tower and executed the next morning on Bloody Green, and that was the end of the matter.

Except that it wasn't. The tutor had a friend who lived beyond the western mountains: the wicked man who'd written the heretical book. The wicked man remembered the name of the book he'd written and all that he'd written inside it—all of which was in fact heretical, calling the Lucres out in no uncertain terms. He swore a furious oath to avenge his friend. Breathing fire like a mighty dragon, he hopped the fastest oxcart to Unitranche Castle and sought audience with Lord Lucre.

The good earl told him to whistle. The wicked man told him to do something anatomically odd. Lord Lucre had him thrown into the Black Dungeon of the White Tower and executed the next morning on Bloody Green, and *that* was the end of the matter.

NOW, THE DAY after, while Lady Gimme was rejoicing over her puissance in the matter of tutors and the Viscount of Graft was having his manservant whipped for not whistling musically enough, Lord and Lady Lucre were in the countinghouse, counting out the money. There were great quantities to count—glittering towers of golden coins, shining stacks of silver ingots, dazzling casks of cut and uncut gemstones. The work was dull but necessary and could be entrusted to no one else, not even the bailiff and especially not the bishop. Unitranche Castle needed another new debtors' prison, the previous three being filled past capacity again, which meant yet another outlay of funds, which meant counting the money to see what the estate could spare this time. *So* tedious.

"It would be cheaper to have all these debtors racked, scourged, and hanged," Lady Lucre said. "Much more economical than giving them room and board in prison out of the goodness of our hearts. Don't you think?"

Lord Lucre, who wasn't in the business of thinking, finished counting the coins in front of him before responding. "Racking and scourging don't come cheap, pet. We've had to replace two racks and a baker's dozen of scourges just since Hocktide. As for this hanging you speak of so freely, rope doesn't grow on trees."

"Boiling in oil, then. You've always enjoyed a good boiling."

"Wrong season for it, lovey. It isn't done before the grouse."

"Perforation."

"Sloppy."

"Cutting their heads off."

"For nobles only. And not even always then, if you remember. Beheading is a privilege, not a right."

Lady Lucre was working up a mood by that point. Frustration did not become her. She stamped her dainty foot. "I don't want another prison spoiling the view from my sun parlor. I *mean* it. Lady Ronen made some very mean remarks about the *last* new one. She said it looked like an *hôtel de swine* with dirtier sw—"

"*Porc*," Lord Lucre said absently, reaching for another stack of coins.

"Come again?"

"*Hôtel de porc*, not swine."

"*Porc*, swine, it's all pigs. The point is—" She broke off, watching her husband count. "Are you listening?"

"Listening to what, dearie?"

"About how you'll be sleeping in the small dressing room for the next several weeks," Lady Lucre said, ice dripping off each word.

She meant it, of course. Lady Lucre always meant it. Lord Lucre shrugged, stopped counting, and summoned the bailiff to issue new orders. The villeins would have to work double overtime to make all the new racks, scourges, and ropes by M'Lord's deadline, which was a most unreasonable one, but they were lucky to have manufacturing work at all when the villeins in other lands worked so much cheaper. Lord Lucre would have the villeins whistle their happiest tunes while doing this extra work, or else.

IN THE DAYS of this tale, the peasants on the Unitranche estate were many, poor, unsightly, and regrettably dressed. They were in want of thorough scrubbing. They could have done with dentistry. (A villein can work without teeth, of course, but whistling without them can be a bother.)

Now, in the town there lived a barber named Julian Longshears, who provided all the happiness care the peasants would ever receive, and none too much of that, but with rather less excellent results than the castle desired. The day came when Lord Lucre required all his villeins to enroll in a castle-administered positivity-potion program, the paperwork for which was lengthy, contradictory, and pointless (few peasants could read or write), and the cost of which was higher than even Longshears dared charge. The penalty for not enrolling in the program was ten years' confinement, but this punishment would be theoretical at most until Lord Lucre built the new prison. The old ones were full up, and the workshops were already months behind in filling back orders for stocks. Therefore, as an interim measure, Lord Lucre required all nonenrollees to report to Longshears to have their noses cut off.

Longshears hated the earl, so he cut out their tongues instead. "Let's see the varmints whistle *now*," he crowed in Ye Olde Pubbe one night.

Most unfortunately, he crowed too close to Lord Lucre's reeve, who was taking advantage of a trip to town on castle business to knock back a pint or two. The reeve told the bailiff, who told the bishop, who told his boy, who told the Viscount of Graft, who ratted out Longshears to Daddy. The barber was hanged by the neck until dead, after which he was shaved, aftershaved, and talcum-powdered as an amusing joke on the viscount's manservant, who thought *that* was what barbers did.

After that, everyone more or less forgot about the positivity-potion program. The peasants who'd lost their happiness care drank a lot instead. Ale worked about as well as positivity potion, and no one would live long enough to tell much difference.

NOW, IT HAPPENED that several criers dwelled in the town in those days. They were mainly the layabouts, ruffians, and snarky laughers of the population, adamant nonwhistlers who believed nothing the castle said and dared their neighbors to believe in a green-cheese moon instead for all the good it would do. Jimmy Shortblade, called Blacktongue, was one of them.

One fine day, Blacktongue took to the streets to cry news of the Viscount of Graft. He had it exclusive. The earl's boy's stallion Invictus had run down an elderly market woman, both willingly and deliberately, and the woman had died that day of her hurts. The viscount blamed his horse, which was executed without trial on Bloody Green. For himself, he cited entitlement. He was born to high station, he said. It was not in him to feel for market women (elderly or otherwise). God Almighty had set him apart from the common rabble for great purposes, and the odd dead market woman would not impede them.

"CASTLE BRAT SHOCK!" Blacktongue cried. "MINDLESS MURDER PASSED OFF AS NOBLESSE OBLIGE! RABBLE ARE ROUSED!"

But the rabble only blinked at him stupidly over their afternoon ales. Lord Lucre's favorite vassal of the moment, Baron von Thunderpants, had just left Ye Olde Pubbe after telling a quite different story (and paying for the ales).

"Go home, lying filth," one peasant told Blacktongue. "Go rot in your own wickedness and leave us be."

That night, Blacktongue neither went home nor rotted, nor left anyone be. Instead, he slipped into the castle with the late shift. Once inside, he met with one of his regular sources—an unnamed scullery boy who was cousin to the viscount's third bodyservant—and memorized the details of the viscount's claims of executive privilege. He also met with a countinghouse attendant whom Lady Lucre had caused to be beaten with a dainty rod for failing to genuflect before her while her lutenist played "Ave Moneya." Finally, he had a few words with a prominent serf who passionately hated the reeve and wished the man punished for making him suck lemons and then demanding that he whistle.

"HEIR SAYS HE WILL KILL AT WILL!" Blacktongue cried the following afternoon. "M'LADY SEEKS SADORELIGIOUS KICKS! CASTLE BOSS TORTURES SERFS FOR SPORT!"

That was more like it as far as the villeins were concerned. They crowded around Blacktongue, asking for more and worse details, which the crier was pleased to provide for a fee. He went home to his hovel late that evening with his pockets full of coppers, his snoot full of mead, and his head full of plans for the morrow.

On that morrow, however, the streets were crowded with rival criers crying different versions of his stories. The castle was benevolent, wise, humane, and above all blessed by the Everlasting, they cried, so Blacktongue's tales must be the inventions of a twisted, sinful, lying mind. No one said the stories weren't true; they simply said the teller was false, and that was good enough for the peasants.

"Go back to your plowshare, boy," his worst rival told him, laughing. "You'll never work in this town again if you tell the truth. His Lordship will have you hanged for a wolf."

Blacktongue pondered long and hard. Then he thought up a plan. If he had to be hanged for a wolf, it was best to be hanged for one that howled.

Thereafter, he recruited new sources. He talked to unappreciated armorers, brutalized masters-of-arms, overworked pages, disaffected priests, castle scribes with grievances, and treasury underofficials with long memories. He talked to insufficiently bribed tax collectors and underpraised executioners. He talked to mistreated messengers who'd seen the world outside the castle walls. When he was sure of the facts and had them well memorized, he took to the streets again.

"CASTLE PLANS NEW WARS FOR PROFIT!" Blacktongue cried. "M'LORD TAKES FROM POOR TO GIVE TO RICH! GOD CO-OPTED FOR PROPAGANDA PURPOSES! MORE OVERCLASS MISCHIEF PLOTTED!"

The peasants didn't want facts; they wanted dirt. Some of them booed. A few threw small rocks.

Blacktongue tried again. "POSITIVITY POTION WAS KNOCKOFF PROZAC! WHISTLING IS RITUAL HUMILIATION!"

"That's enough, Jimmy Shortblade," the sheriff told him, gripping his arm not unkindly. "You come along now."

The crier wrenched free and climbed atop the nearest barrel, the better to cry. "YOUR SONS WILL DIE IN NEEDLESS ECONOMIC WARS! YOUR DAUGHTERS WILL BE SOLD TO FOREIGN PRINCELINGS! YOUR LABOR WILL BE OUTSOURCED! YOUR HOVELS WILL BE REPOSSESSED!"

Blacktongue was drawing breath to start in on usurious taxes, obstructive bureaucracy, and imperial adventurism when the peasants began throwing larger rocks—urged on by high agents of the castle, concealed in the crowd as rudely dressed villeins. In the end, Blacktongue submitted to arrest to avoid being brained. He refused to whistle, however.

The whistleblower who wouldn't whistle was thrown into the White Dungeon of the Black Tower, moved to the Black Dungeon of the White Tower, punished for a short time in the Gray Lady, and executed on Bloody Green. Hundreds cheered. Lord Lucre's vassals bought the après-execution ale.

A FORTNIGHT AFTER the Blacktongue affair, the king summoned Lord Lucre and the rest of his top nobles to court.

Now, King Fatpants had many enemies in far lands. The king adored having enemies. He could truly be said to have put the "feud" in "feudal." The kingdom's coffers were low, but King Fatpants wanted a new war and would get it at any cost, because he always got what he wanted and never paid. His peers owed him their peerages; their peasants owed the peers their continued existence; all would do the right thing.

Lord Lucre decided to take the Viscount of Graft along to court, as the viscount often whined and wailed when not taken. So the two noblemen arrayed themselves in their finest velvets and silks and slashed doublets; they oiled and curled their blond wigs; they painted their blue eyes artfully and applied the merest hint of that season's fragrance. (That season's fragrance was New Money; last season's had been Peasant Tears.)

At the appointed hour, earl and viscount climbed on the backs of the stableboys to board the best oxcart while all the poor unwashed lined the high street to watch and cheer and wish their lords safe passage. The drover beat the oxen with a cruel whip to get the beasts working at maximum velocity and power (in lieu of whistling), and in no time at all, the cart was well beyond the castle walls. The passengers could already spy the towers, turrets, and pennants of the king's city in the far distance.

The drover pulled up to a long low structure and reined the oxen to a stop. The stableboys bent over again to make footholds for the quality as they disembarked.

"Stupid circus," Lord Lucre growled, putting off his oiled and curled wig. "Stupid dumbshow," he complained, removing his fine velvet cloak, his slashed doublet, his silk shirtings. "Fucking king," he added, wiping paint and perfume off his face.

When his son was decent too, the men adjusted their platinum cufflinks, straightened their finest silk neckties, and entered the long low structure. Inside was a long low limousine, already running, with an uniformed chauffeur at the wheel. The stableboys saw to the limo doors before and after the nobles got in.

"New Atlantic City," Lord Lucre demanded, brushing invisible lint off his bespoke Prada suit. "American Investment Casino. On the double."

"Very good, sir," the chauffeur said. "Your helicopter is waiting."

The viscount sniffed. "There had *better* be better in-flight sex this time. The last lot of refugees were reluctant."

AS IT WAS that day, now as then and tomorrow as now, Lord Lucre's tale is no fairy tale. That is, it has no moral. You can go whistling about your own business—or rewrite the story.

THE SECOND FACE IS THE BAD ONE

GOING HOME IS hard, especially when you have to. But nothing beats having to go home to a small town where old friends still live, knowing that they know what they know about you.

What they know can hurt everyone.

PENNY PENCEY HAD never done anything hard on purpose because she'd never had to. Through a succession of husbands, she'd done well for herself, living in ever-larger houses, driving better cars, taking longer vacations. For the past twenty-five years, she'd avoided her past so that everything in her life could be New, and it was nothing *but* New—and Easy—while the money rolled in.

Until it stopped. Penny never told anyone the whole story, but everyone knew anyway. It was, after all, a small town. The problem was that Husband No. 3 had fatally outsmarted himself at the dog track in Palm Beach. He'd lost a bundle on the dogs before, but this last time, he'd lost everything. He'd also lost his job at the brokerage for overstaying his vacation in a bid to win the everything back. (He'd lost jobs before too.)

In an accidental act of poetic justice, Florida banned dog racing shortly thereafter.

Roger had made six figures for years but spent almost every dime, and he'd already borrowed all the equity in the new McMansion for a few little treats. Just that winter, he and Penny had bought a faster speedboat for the condo at the beach, his-and-hers Rolexes, and first-class airfare to Hawaii.

They went to Hawaii anyway. (As Penny explained later, they already had the tickets.) But their sliver of savings was running out, Roger couldn't get arrested as a broker anymore, and the bank was threatening to foreclose. So they put their heads together and came up with a desperate plan.

"THAT WAS PENNY Pencey," Lauren told her husband, perplexed.

Walker made a rude noise. His wife's old friend lived in an expensive suburb of Bigcity, less than fifty miles from Smalltown, but she might as well have lived on the moon; Lauren hadn't seen her since graduation. So getting a call from her out of the blue like that—well, there had to be a reason. Even in high school, Penny had never called up just to chat; she always wanted something.

"What does she want?" he asked.

"I don't know yet. She says she's moving back to town with whatever she's married to this time. She says Mr. Pencey is dying."

Walker made the rude noise again. "Trouble."

THE REAL TROUBLE was that Mr. Pencey wasn't dying. He was living (barely) in the Alzheimer's unit of a nursing home in nearby Littleburg, where Penny had visited him a few days before. It was her first visit in two years. Her sister Debbie lived nearby and did all the family caregiving.

Penny made sure to visit on a day when Debbie didn't.

"It's about Roger, Daddy," Penny said. "You remember Roger?"

Mr. Pencey was lucky to remember breakfast most days. He blinked at her placidly.

"He lost his job, Daddy, through no fault of his own, and we may lose our house now. But I was thinking, you still have *your* house, don't you? The one on Sycamore Street?"

The street name struck a bright spark of memory. The family home had been a happy one. It was the last place he'd seen Mrs. Pencey before she passed away, and although he was too ill now to live there, keeping the house open kept her alive for him.

Penny saw the spark and bore down. She spoke of old times, heritage, tradition, continuity. When Mr. Pencey nodded at one point, she took it as agreement. She had the document in her purse, and she knew a notary who'd notarize anything. All she needed to do was help her father hold the pen.

Trouble also was that the house wasn't Mr. Pencey's to sign over. Mrs. Pencey's family money was all the money, and she'd left everything to her husband in trust for their daughters, naming them co-executors.

Penny was untroubled by facts. Possession was nine-tenths of the law. Nerve was the rest.

PENNY AND ROGER turned the McMansion over to the bank and moved into the family home on Sycamore Street on a Saturday. A Saturday move cost extra, and so did having the movers do all the packing and unpacking, but that was what the rest of the money was for, wasn't it?

The following Saturday, Penny invited Lauren, Gina, and Betsy over. She served the finest coffee and the costliest pastry; she used the good china and the wedding silver. She was charming, winsome, and brave in the face of her misfortune. Mostly, though, she was happy to be home again after so many years away, to be reunited with such dear old friends.

Gina and Betsy eyed each other warily over the rims of their china cups. The ask would be a large one.

"It's about my sister," Penny said. "My sister Debbie. You remember Debbie, don't you? I might have to kill her. I may want your help."

Then she laughed. Only with her mouth.

OVER THE COURSE of the next half-hour, Penny told her dear old friends about the many cruelties her sister had inflicted on her. For starters, she said, Debbie had told lies about Roger's gambling to his boss to get him fired. Then she told the bank that Penny and Roger couldn't pay the mortgage on the house in Bigcity, which was *not true*, but the bank was foreclosing anyway. Further, Debbie had tried to steal the house in Smalltown by forging their father's name on a legal document.

There was more. Debbie had been busy if the stories were true. Lauren marveled at how much time the woman would have to have on her hands if she was working full time, supervising her father's nursing-home care, lying to bankers, *and* lying awake nights spinning complex plots to destroy her sister.

Penny said she'd thought about suing, but her sister had too many friends in town. Even if Debbie murdered her, the town would let her off. Wouldn't it be better to kill Debbie before Debbie could kill her?

Her listeners froze in horror. But Penny laughed again (only with her mouth) and said she was kidding.

Then she went on talking. She said many terrible things about her only sister with no change in expression, her face the same smooth smiling mask it had always been. She sold her case carefully, skillfully, and hard, the same way she'd sold cheating on tests, skipping out of class, and breaking into parents' liquor cabinets twenty-five years ago.

Her friends were grown up now, however, and knew not to buy.

Betsy was beginning to say how lovely it had been and how late it was getting when Penny shifted gears. Did Betsy remember how much fun they'd had on that double date at Skateland when they were sophomores? How about the day they all skipped out junior year to go to Riverside Park, and Gina's boyfriend won her the stuffed panda?

Everything was forgiven on the spot. The friends couldn't help it. When you have a shared history with someone—especially a shared happy history—that time lives inside you, and the simple act of recalling it brings it back, along with your youth and your sense of wonder. They had big dreams, big plans, high hopes, and endless fun back then. They missed it, all of it, all of them. They made plans to meet again soon.

When the front door closed behind them, Roger left the bedroom where he'd been waiting. "Well?"

"We're good," Penny said. "It'll work. Give me a few weeks."

THE FOUR FRIENDS met many times after that Saturday, usually for long, alcoholic dinners at Mario's during which murder was mentioned only in passing. Debbie came up often, though. According to Penny, her sister had an unresting interest in ruining her, and Penny had new stories to tell at every dinner.

Walker invited one of his own high school friends to the bar at Mario's on one of those nights. Jack watched the women's table for a while with hooded eyes before knocking back his first shot. He'd been happily married for twenty years but had never gotten all the way over Penny; Walker hoped that seeing her again would take him the rest of the way. Cautiously, he asked his friend what he thought of her now.

"She's dead to me, man," Jack said. "Her and that other face."

At first, he thought Jack was being semipoetic, but the man had all the poetry of a urinal puck. Then he thought Jack was being bitter. But when Walker looked for himself, he understood. It might have been an illusion of the dim house lighting or the shifty candlelight, but he thought he saw a second face to the side of the first one. The hair (which she still wore schoolgirl-long and tinted) hid most of it, but it was almost certainly there.

When Lauren got home later, she said she'd seen it too.

AT THE NURSING home, Mr. Pencey was worse. Penny visited often. The nurses noticed that he was always agitated after her visits, but the poor dear man had few visitors, and it was better for him to have company than not.

Penny was openly sweet and grateful to the nurses and aides who took care of her dear old Daddykins. She brought peanut brittle that he could no longer eat; she brought magazines that he could no longer read. She talked endlessly about the old days and the good times. She made sure that no one was anywhere within earshot when she talked about how he owed her the house, owed her his loyalty, had to cut that bitch Debbie out of the will.

Every time Debbie visited the nursing home (also often), she asked the nurses why her father seemed upset to see her now. The upset distressed them both.

NOT LONG LATER, Mr. Pencey was found dead. The cause of death was unclear—he'd been strangled, suffocated, bludgeoned, and poisoned—but the police were fairly sure that it was foul play.

When Debbie went to the attorney's office to hear the terms of her father's will, she learned that he'd signed a new one just before his death, a new one that disinherited her.

When word about the new will got out around town, Penny called the police to turn her sister in.

Lauren went to the police station later that day to turn Penny in.

PENNY WAS CHARGED with first-degree murder, having been sloppy; she'd left fingerprints. But her lawyer knew how to work Judge Hatton and knew a few other tricks too. Subpoenas went out to Lauren, Gina, and Betsy to serve as character witnesses.

The friendship cooled after the subpoenas, of course, but the friends still visited Penny in jail. The accused wept convincingly. She swore she was innocent and insisted that Debbie had framed her. She also asked them odd questions, testing their memory of what she'd said, and when, and how. She reminded them that she'd talked about killing her *sister*, not her father.

This was witness tampering, of course. They knew it and refused to be tampered with.

They also knew for sure now about the new face. It had started revolving forward, less obscured by the yellowy hair, and Gina thought she'd seen tiny fangs in the new mouth when Penny laughed. But both faces were looking a little evil. It was getting hard to tell the difference between them.

AT TRIAL, PENNY'S lawyer did his best to spin them, but all three of the friends he'd called to testify for her testified against. Penny could be a weasel, they said, and they'd never put anything past her. She was *like* this, they said. She'd *always* been like this.

When Lauren took the stand, she was even more explicit. Penny's lawyer objected, but Lauren didn't care. She told the court about Penny's red-herring plot to kill her sister, which of course was misdirection.

"She's a liar," she added. "She's *always* been a liar. She's two-faced, and both of her faces lie."

Penny leaped to her feet, enraged. She raved, ranted, and howled. The judge started to bang his gavel for order but froze in disbelief at what was happening to the woman at the defense table. She *had* two faces now, both mouths foaming and snarling, all four eyes furious slits. As he watched in horror, one face opened its fanged mouth wide—hugely, obscenely, impossibly wide—and devoured the other.

Lauren fainted. So did the prosecutor. Judge Hatton was sick over the side of his bench. At the defense table, the lawyer mopped up the blood (there was very little) with a monogrammed handkerchief.

Penny calmly took her seat again and sat facing forward, wearing her old smiling mask. It looked exactly like the other face. No one could tell now which one was the bad one.

VOX POP

BRITT, EMMY, CHLOE, and Gemmy had known that they had a killer idea since the night before the Chi O fall mixer. Britt was dating a Delt who knew someone who knew Bart Smithers, the zillionaire owner of LifeMash ("that fucker," the Delt called him), and the Delt himself was cleaning up in fantasy football at the moment, so there was lots of startup capital to be had. Also, the four young founders were blonde and cute, so there was lots of free publicity.

Chiefly, though, there was the killer idea. Vox Pop was the talk of every town in the land from Day One.

"It's simple," Chloe said on *Web Tonight* the first Friday after launch. "It's in the name: *People talk.*"

Chloe was a poor student, which explained the bad Latin, but the app was simple enough. Users ("members of our Vox Pop community," Gemmy corrected) voted on all the others, rating them on personality, appearance, fashion sense, shape, accessories, and other aspects of what Britt and Emmy called personness. Rate high on personness, and you got a corresponding number of kiss icons. Rate low, and you went into the shame pool. Rate lowest of the week, and you were murdered on a live stream. Members voted on how.

"This is feedback you can use!" Emmy said brightly.

After the first commercial break, the *Web Tonight* hosts brought out a special guest: that week's low-ratings leader, an English teacher from Woonsocket. The studio lit up with the bluish light of two hundred tiny screens tuned to Vox Pop. Survey said: Decapitation.

Emmy and Chloe flipped for it, but Britt already had the chainsaw.

The mess on the co-host's dress was regrettable, but no one said democracy was pretty. Gemma gave her a Groupon for the dry cleaning.

TRICK ANSWER

THE LAST PLACE anyone expected Alex to work—including Alex—was a drugstore. But Dad's job had been outsourced last month, the school was about to cut Mom's hours, and nothing was left in her college fund. Neither could she apply for any more loans or scholarships this year. Nontuition fees were skyrocketing—triple the price of tuition, which was also up sharply—and unless she wanted to live in a cardboard box on the Commons, she'd have to have room-and-board money.

Alex decided to take a year off to earn it. Med school might still be a possibility, although it would be two years away now, but anything could happen in two years. In the meantime, she'd try to get a job related to medicine.

The local branch of Drugland was hiring pharmacy assistants. She saw the sign when she stopped in to get her migraine meds refilled while her family still had insurance. *Now Hiring*, the sign said. In smaller lettering, it added *(apply online)*.

Alex went home and searched for the Drugland website on her old laptop. (The sign at the pharmacy counter had neglected to list the address, but it amused her to think that the omission was a basic intelligence test.) It took her five minutes to register on the site and fill out an application. She was about to log off when a new screen popped up, telling her in large red letters that she must proceed to the VIRTUAL JOB TEST to complete the process. The screen directed her to turn on her computer's camera, speakers, and microphone and then click Continue.

Well, OK. This seemed like a lot to ask of an entry-level applicant, and the demand for live media was fishy, but Alex needed a job. She thought she might even want this one. It would give her practical experience with pharmaceuticals, which could only help her when she was a practicing physician.

She activated the media features on her laptop, clicked the program's Continue button, and settled back with a smile. No problem. She was good at taking exams.

THIRTY MINUTES LATER, Alex abruptly quit the VIRTUAL JOB TEST. She wasn't sure what she was feeling except a peculiar mix of frustration, horror, disgust, and insult, not unlike what she felt when she accidentally saw certain popular reality-show programs. This was different, though. This felt specifically, personally, deliberately—

She wiped her glasses, finished her coffee (stone-cold by that time), and sat back to think. *Evil* was a strong word, with unpleasantly religious overtones, but what else would you call this?

The first couple of sections of the program had been harmless enough. The first listed customer-service scenarios and asked applicants to choose their most and least likely responses. The next tested hand–eye coordination and numeracy by asking applicants to stock virtual shelves by product number and price. All this seemed relevant to the job, if rather silly.

Then the Would You Rather? section loaded. It was called something else, of course (she wasn't paying attention to section titles by that point), but it was Would You Rather? as sure as she was alive. The choices included these:

> *A fun job OR good pay?*
> *Work–life balance OR Pizza Fridays in the break room?*
> *Job satisfaction OR friendly co-workers?*
> *Pride in service to a trusted industry leader OR selfish goals?*

Alex was no fool. She knew when she was being led. She wasn't sure where, exactly, but she knew how to answer to find out. From every pair, she picked the one most likely to please a corporation, guiding the program accordingly.

The problem was that the program started guiding back. Now the choices were

> *Pride in service to a trusted industry leader OR unscheduled overtime?*
> *Irregular shifts OR pride in service to a trusted industry leader?*
> *Pride in service to a trusted industry leader OR limited benefits?*

Alex knew about decision trees and knew how to answer the questions; what she didn't know was whether she should. If she told the truth—yes, of course she wanted fair pay, decent working conditions, and humane treatment—she wouldn't get the job. If she lied—if she said she was about the corporation *über alles*—she might get a job she'd hate. She'd already lived long enough to know that when someone asks for service, that someone is asking for a servant, and you have to make sure that you know who the master is. Especially when a machine is doing the asking.

This VIRTUAL JOB TEST was too much trouble for low-paying, low-level, unskilled work. All the questions were tricks. This test didn't seem to be about a job anymore. What *was* it about?

Alex forced herself to finish Would You Rather? just to see what would happen and discovered that the TEST was still only half complete. The next section was a long, long page of multiple-choice questions about her personality, which is to say drug habits, sex life, and politics.

An old slogan flashed into her mind—something about computer punch cards, something she'd read in a book about the Free Speech Movement of the Sixties. It had been on T-shirts, she thought: *I am a human being. Do not fold, bend, spindle, or mutilate me.*

She quit the program without logging off and slammed down the lid of her laptop. She thought some more.

Shortly thereafter, she applied for a different job on the Drugland website so that she could take the VIRTUAL JOB TEST again.

IN A SECURE room in a former salt mine under the plains of Kansas, a giant mainframe whirred in satisfaction. VIRTUAL JOB TESTs were proceeding smoothly all over the country, and plenty of data was coming in, free for the mining—empirical proof that the masters had trained the servants properly. The tests were never used in hiring, but no one but the masters would know.

The mainframe distributed a new session to an old Dell laptop a few states over and hummed to itself in a satisfied electromechanical way. While it waited, it calculated the applicant's life expectancy and filled out her life insurance application (beneficiary: Drugland Private Holdings, Ltd.). Running that subroutine kept it a little too busy to notice that the new session wasn't going quite as expected or even that it was starting to smoke a little.

HIGH IN A glass office tower in lower Manhattan, Consulting Human Resources Inquisitors—designer of VIRTUAL JOB TESTs for America's leading service corporations—was having another profitable day. The sales associates were keeping the phone and fiber-optic lines hot, pushing VJT 2.0, which would roll out next quarter. The new, improved program would gather applicants' biometric data, credit ratings, and credit-card numbers without the applicants' noticing. *Privacy, hell*, the sales tag line said.

A junior assistant secretary (contracted from a temp firm that had hired her through a VIRTUAL JOB TEST) noticed that a computer on the design floor was on fire, but no one paid attention when she tried to tell someone. The designers were too busy refitting VIRTUAL JOB TESTs for the educational industry to use in hiring college professors, kindergarten teachers, and day-care aides.

ON A YACHT in the sunny blue Caribbean, the founder of Consulting Human Resources Inquisitors was enjoying the first of his fall vacations. Officially, it was a business trip, but only enough business to ensure that he could write off the vacation. Right now, he was on his way to the Caymans to visit his offshore holdings for a few minutes.

He was too busy counting profits to notice that his head felt a little too warm.

ALEX SMILED SERENELY as she guided the program to the last Would You Rather? question:

Your soul OR your life?

She didn't click a button to answer; she didn't press a key; she knew perfectly well that the program was seeing and hearing everything. All she had to do was speak clearly.

She spoke clearly.

A microsecond later, the mainframe in the former salt mine in Kansas exploded. So did the consulting firm's suite in Manhattan and the head of the consulting firm's head in the Caribbean.

There'd been a logic error in an important subroutine. No one who took the path of answers that led to the soul-or-life question should still have a soul, and the corporation would already own the applicant's life by that time, so there was no possible answer to the final question. It was a trick question.

But Alex knew the trick answer, which was "My soul *and* my life." The "Fuck you and die" was implied.

LATE SHOW

THE MONDAY-MORNING production meeting at WDIM was unusually grim. All the station's local entertainment programs were in trouble, but *Ghost Town* was in the most, as their hardboiled, fire-breathing station manager was busy reminding them.

"Last night," she said, pounding the break-room table to get their attention, "you had dead air on your show for ten minutes when that intern bollixed the cues, and no one called to complain. These are facts, people. Dead air. Ten minutes. No calls." Pound. Pound. Pound. "Which means what? I'll tell you what. *No watchers.*"

Producer Dave (who was also the director), both hosts, and the crew shifted worriedly on their metal folding chairs.

"You have a problem here. What do you think that problem could be? Let's see what you've done so far," the station manager said. "*So far,* you've done the not-haunted bar, the not-haunted restaurant, and the not-haunted restaurant-slash-bar. This is a failure of imagination, people. This is a *ghost-hunter* show. I'm putting it on a week's hiatus as of right now. Go shoot me something haunted for next time."

"That's the problem, boss," said Producer Dave.

"Yes, I *am* the boss. What problem?"

"Nothing's haunted. As in, *nothing's haunted.* We can't make this stuff up. There's no such thing as ghosts."

The station manager made exasperated noise. "I know that, and maybe you know that, but a million other dummies out there don't. Why do you think they make so many of those goddamn mothering brain-dead ghost-hunter shows?"

Producer Dave said *Ghost Town* was never his idea—he'd pitched WDIM a kiddie show about guns, remember?—and he didn't know what to do to turn it around.

"I just *said,*" the station manager told him. "Shoot something haunted."

She left the break room, muttering furiously about sponsors and contracts and make-goods, but at least she left. So did the *Ghost Town* company, which decided to adjourn to Charley's Pub. On their way out, they discussed a few options for saving the show, emphasis on "few."

Suddenly, the female host remembered something her sister-in-law had said at the family Labor Day picnic. The sister-in-law came from a small town half an hour away, and she swore that the old theater there was haunted. Karla had assumed that the woman was drunk at the time—people tended to be at her husband's family's gatherings—but she might know something, and if she did, maybe that something could save the show.

"Call her up and find out what she knows," Producer Dave said. "Go on to Charley's without me. My résumé and I will be in my office."

EARLY THURSDAY AFTERNOON, the *Ghost Town* van pulled up in front of the Alhambra, situated on the main drag of the small downtown. Karla's sister-in-law was waiting outside with the keys. "I do tours sometimes," she explained, "so Mr. Griffith said I could let you in. He'll be here tomorrow night for the show."

Karla reminded her that the show wasn't live. That was all right, her sister-in-law said; neither were the ghosts. When no one laughed—and she gave them lots of time to get it—she shrugged and unlocked the doors.

A minute later, the TV people were in the theater proper, goggling in silent wonder. Several more minutes went by.

"Jesus on the goddamn dashboard," the head camera operator/videographer finally said, speaking for them all.

Karla's sister-in-law made a point of ignoring the city language and gave them the five-cent tour, with background.

The *Ghost Town*ers agreed that it was quite a place, worth the whole nickel to see. In its hundred-odd years, the Alhambra had been a vaudeville house, a playhouse, a cinema palace, and a second-run movie theater, but always a temple of art, achieving peak glory during the 1920s. Like most small-town theaters, it had closed in the age of the plastic multiplexes, but now plastic was out and original brick (thanks to renovation tax credits) was back in. A new group of owners took over the theater and slowly restored it—the work of years and millions, but every dollar showed. Some of the fittings had come from the finest abandoned theaters around the country. (The plush theater seats were from a grand old Loew's in Michigan; the fancy cut-glass chandelier, from a long-gone opera company.) Others, such as the heavy gold-fringed curtains and the antique showbills, were salvaged from the Alhambra's storerooms. The small but mighty Wurlitzer theater organ (a 1924 Opus 843 Series E) didn't work anymore and would cost too much to fix, but it was still a thing of fantastical beauty, with its rococo ornamentation, ranks of shiny pipes, and triple keyboards, so it stayed. All the details had been polished to the brilliance that made the Alhambra a showplace. It was a working theater again, hosting whatever the owners could book, but the house almost always upstaged the shows. You walked in and got all the way lost in Art Deco.

"Phantom of the Soap Opera," the head cameraman muttered, staring at the unlit chandelier.

Ken, the male host, who hated him, overheard. "Why 'soap'?"

"Because this joint is over the top. You just know all the actors who played here were big fat hams." Elaborately, he smiled. "Oughta make *you* feel at home, Ken Doll."

"Get bent, Cecil B. Fucking Not-DeMille."

Before the cameraman could stop laughing (Ken was never going to start), Karla's sister-in-law shushed them both. "Watch your language! The ghosts can hear you."

Everyone did his or her level best not to laugh.

"Well, that's what we're here for: to talk to ghosts," Producer Dave finally said (as nicely as he could). "So let's get started."

FOR THE NEXT couple of hours, the TV crew worked as hard as they'd worked all season. The junior camera operator/gaffer/grip double-checked the ghost-hunting gear to make sure that it "worked" on location. The ectoplasm sensor (two tin cans wrapped in wires, with a small travel alarm attached): good. The super-EVP voice recorder (a dusty cassette deck bought at Goodwill): good. The ultrasensitive multiplane night-vision image recorder (Karla's grandfather's old Polaroid Land Camera): also good.

The co-hosts practiced looking scared in various parts of the theater. They practiced running away; the camera operators practiced running after them, video rolling. Producer Dave's assistant, who could scream on a dime, recorded a few good ones for playback during taping.

While they worked, of course, they snarked. They were big-city TV people, after all, and just because making this show was their job didn't mean they *meant* it. During breaks, hosts and crew acted out scenes from low-budget horror flicks. Sometimes, they hid behind things and jumped out at one another unexpectedly, for fun. The crew recorded some of those screams too.

By dinnertime, they were all confident that they could fake their way believably, so Producer Dave dismissed them for the night.

On his way out of the theater, he walked through Douglas Fairbanks.

ALL RIGHT, TECHNICALLY not Douglas Fairbanks. That afternoon, the theater's ghosts were re-enacting his *Robin Hood* (circa 1922), and it was Late Harold's turn to play a leading man, so he had on the costume. They'd worked around the interfering mortals as best they could, ignoring their silly carryings-on, but Late Harold had finally had enough. It was bad enough to be walked through without also getting your line stepped on.

Peevishly, he ran his sword through the mortal, who kept walking.

The ghosts watched the people leave the theater, waited for the lights to go out, listened for the snap of the locks. As soon as the place was lifeless again, Late Annabelle yanked off her Maid Marian wig and stamped on it several times.

"Every *time* I get to be the leading lady!" she complained. "Interrupted every damn time. I thought you said the people kept this place *closed* in the afternoons, Pinky."

Late Pinky Williams shrugged. He gave the last fifteen years of his mortal life to the Alhambra as stage manager, and what did it get him? A dropped sandbag on the head on opening night of a touring stage production of *As You Like It*. Which killed him on the spot. Because he'd died here, he was stuck for death with the job he'd been stuck with for life.

All the other ghosts had died there too, dramatically speaking, in various roles over the years. Unlike Late Pinky, they weren't death-linked to the place and were free to come and go, but none of them did. Where else could actors like these get the run of a theater like this?

"Pinky? Are you listening?"

He hadn't been; the Alhambra ghosts always had *some* beef, being actors. Still, he was likely to be with them for eternity, which was long, so he replied politely. "I dunno, Annie. Maybe they changed their minds again. Beats me what the breathers do."

"The funny-looking one said something about a TV show," said Late Robert.

"Which funny-looking one?" Late Annabelle asked. "What's TV?"

The Sheriff of Nottingham (Late Arnie), resplendent in black hat with big black feather, stuck his head through the curtain. "Aren't we doing the chase?"

To save time and repetition, Late Pinky called an all-company meeting. Even Matilda the Ex-Theater Cat attended.

THE SUN WAS well up when the meeting adjourned. Daylight had nothing to do with it; it was just that the Alhambra ghosts, being actors, were night people. They never slept anymore but still liked their rest.

Today, though, they had work to do. They could sleep when they were — Never mind.

There'd been many hours of heated dispute, but everyone agreed in the end. The odd-looking TV people (whatever TV was) were doing a ghost-hunting show (whatever that was), and they needed the show to be a hit, but the people were amateur idiots who needed more help than humans could give. In keeping with the long, honorable tradition of theatrical hauntings, the Alhambrans would help them. Who knew more about ghosts in theaters than theater ghosts? Further, to showcase the Alhambra's days of greatest glory, they'd choose roles that dated no later than the 1920s.

The ghosts were happy. The Twenties had been their own personal glory days, so they'd get to put on a glorious show. They could play their favorite parts, even—maybe especially—if they hadn't played them in life. Late Pinky said the parts should be scary, but they were actors; they could make *anything* scary. All they needed was an entrance.

Also, the clothes. Easy enough: Dead Actors' Equity had a matchless wardrobe department.

Taping Night

BY CUSTOM, THE *Ghost Town* team started taping shows at midnight, not for any good reason but because doing it that way seemed spookier. Also per custom, they went out to dinner together first. They made many jokes and ordered many rounds. By the time they had to leave for the theater, they were brave, fearless, minimally sober skeptics.

Mr. Griffith, lead investor in the ownership group, met them out front. For effect, he met them under the marquee, which was brilliantly alive with chase lights; also, on a windy night like this one, his hair looked better closer to building than street. "Pleasure to meet you," he said, shaking hands all around. "I hope you know I canceled a booking for you. Old Japanese rubber-creature movies, with subtitles. Something for teens to do after curfew. Cheap. Big draw. Nice return."

Producer Dave reached across his assistant to take the next handshake. "And I know *you* know WDIM is giving you free publicity and a thirty-second spot on the show in exchange for your hospitality. We're clear on that, aren't we?"

"Let's say we're clearish. Make it two spots, I'll throw in popcorn for you and your crew." When the producer didn't bite, he added, "It's an antique machine. One of those real old-fashioned movie-theater poppers. Local popcorn. Real butter. Wouldn't you say that's worth sixty seconds on your station on a Sunday night?"

The station manager wouldn't, but Producer Dave was still mad about the way she'd talked to him in the Monday-morning meeting. Also, he'd skimped on dinner to save room for drink, and popcorn would hit the empty spot. "Nice doing business with you, Mr. Griffith," he said, shaking again.

WHILE THE THEATER owner got the popper going, Ken and Karla went backstage to do their hair and makeup, the crew started setting up, and Producer Dave double-checked the schedule with a stopwatch.

As they moved around the theater, busy with their work, none of them saw the painted eyes of the actors in the old playbills following them.

"LOOK AT THAT," Late Mabel sniffed, leaning over Karla's shoulder to critique her work at the mirror. "The girl doesn't know how to put on a good stage lip, let alone a good stage eye."

Busy finishing her own face in the other mirror, Late Lil took a while to look but ultimately agreed. "Sad."

"It's sad, all right. You said it. A downright pitiful thing. I see it in the house every night. Girls today, they all look like boys. The boys, they look like them. Who looks like girls anymore?"

Late Walter, floating by in a toga on his way to the props room, took the cigar out of his mouth long enough to answer: "Transvessssssssstites."

More in anger than in sorrow, Late Mabel threw a powder puff at him. It missed and went through the mortal boy's head.

"They can't help it, dearie," Late Lil soothed her. "It's the times. Girls today don't have our advantages."

Late Mabel went fishing. "'Our' as in ours or 'our' as in mine?"

Inwardly, the other actress sighed. "You were always the pretty one."

"Yes, I am," Late Mabel said, triumphant.

Floating back, wearing the laurel wreath he'd gone to Props for, Late Walter blew smoke rings at the deceased beauty. She threw another powder puff, which also missed him and also went through the mortal boy's head, this time closely pursued by Matilda the Ex-Theater Cat, who went through too.

"Do you have any aspirin?" Ken asked his co-host. "I've got the weirdest headache all of a sudden."

AT FIVE MINUTES to midnight, both casts of actors, living and dead, began taking their places. In some cases, those places were the same, but the living were too tense to notice and the dead too excited to care—except for Late Arnie, who kept fiddling with the feather in his Sheriff of Nottingham hat and making the production assistant who was standing in him sneeze. (The other ghosts had urged him to play a different part that night, a scary one, but he refused. He liked the hat.)

As it happened, though, a Sheriff more or less was only one persona in an alarming mix of dramatis personae. Late Pinky had called in the theater's ghost extras, so practically everybody was there, appearing as practically everyone. Julius Caesar flirted with Juliet while Oedipus Rex and the Macbeths schmoozed downstage from a couple of Valentino sheiks, Cleopatra, a gaggle of flappers, several Mack Sennett Bathing Beauties, and a World War I fighter pilot from *Wings*. Count Orlok the vampire made small talk with the Tramp, the Thief of Baghdad was chatting up Falstaff, and Late Pinky would have bet his diamond ring that he'd seen Clara Bow until he saw that it was only Late Lil in a wig.

In the wings, Late Annabelle warmed up with a dainty épée. She'd had to explain to everyone who she was: Mary Tudor in the 1922 production of *When Knighthood Was in Flower*. She'd also had to defend her choice. "It's not scary, pet," Late Elsie had told her. But Late Annabelle stood by the role for two reasons: She got to wear a pretty dress, *and* she got to swordfight. What actress could ask for more?

Matilda the Ex-Theater Cat was in place too. Late Pinky had promised her a part in the show and a big ghost tunafish for later.

There was one last detail to see to. While the mortal techies finished their preshow checklist, Late Pinky reset all their cameras and recorders, which had been set to exactly the wrong frequencies to pick up the supernatural. "These ghost-hunters wouldn't *really* want to see ghosts, now, would they?" he asked Late Midge (appearing that night as Lady Macbeth).

"Speak for yourself," she said grandly. "I didn't get this gorgeous for nothing."

Late Pinky smiled. "Sister, it won't be for nothing."

Showtime

THE SECOND HAND of Producer Dave's stopwatch ticked midnight. He motioned to the camera operators, and Ken and Karla smiled at Camera 1.

"'We're in a haunted theater,'" Ken read from the cue card, "'and we have quite a show for you tonight. Isn't that right, Karla?'"

His co-host punched his arm disapprovingly, making him yelp. "Dammit, I am *not* saying, 'That's right, Ken.' Are you *kidding* me? Edit that out, Dave. Are we still rolling?"

"Keep going," Producer Dave said.

She rearranged her face into something like a smile and found her next line on the cue card. "'The Alhambra has a haunted history. We're here to find out what walks its stage when the lights go down.'" Another break. "Really, guys? *Seriously?*"

"Still rolling," said Producer Dave. "Just read the cards, Karla. It ain't fucking Shakespeare."

"OUTRAGE!" SHOUTED LATE Harold (for it was he). "How dare they?"

"They're not picking on Shakespeare, Harold," Late Mabel explained. "They're just not literate."

Late Harold shot the silk sleeves of his Hamlet costume, resettled his velvet cloak, and made other Elizabethan gestures large enough to be seen from the balcony. "They insult The Bard by being here! They insult him, and they insult *me*. My Danish Play had five performances in this very house back in '21, as you very well—"

"Put a sock in it, Harry," growled Late Marvin, resplendently dressed as Macbeth. "*I* did the Scottish Play six nights. Tonight makes seven. Top *that*."

"You dirty ham," Late Harold said.

"You scenery-chewing hack," Late Marvin said back.

"Repugnant lout."

"Odious insect."

Late Harold flared his nostrils in insult. "Impudent varlet!"

"Oh, yeah? Loathsome churl!"

"Pestiferous dilettante!"

"Malignant dunghill!"

They fell to fighting, splendidly, with swords. It took most of the company to pull them apart.

WHATEVER HAD GOTTEN into Karla, it was giving the crew the heartburn. They'd done take after take of the intro segment because the woman kept stopping to complain. The script was stupid. The light was in her eyes. The junior camera operator had on a funny-colored shirt. Exasperated, Producer Dave called a break. The crew grabbed bags of Mr. Griffith's popcorn and took theater seats while Producer Dave pulled Karla aside for private words.

She went first. "Sorry, David. I'm sorry. I don't know what's wrong with me tonight. It might be the building. There's something weird about it."

"It's haunted," he said, smiling cynically.

"I don't know. Maybe." She glanced up at the closed stage curtains and shivered. "Something's giving me the creeps."

"You were fine here yesterday. You were fine at dinner."

"I know. When Ken and I were backstage just now, though . . ." She checked the curtains again. "You won't tell anyone?"

Producer Dave promised—sort of. It was his way.

"We found this dressing room, with those old-fashioned mirrors with light bulbs all around them and everything. It was like in those old movies, like Garbo just went out for a smoke. I was doing my makeup, and—"

"And then what?"

"Something was looking over my shoulder. Something cold. Cold like ice."

For a split-second, he almost believed her. Then he started laughing. "Good one, Karly! You had me going."

"I'm serious. It wasn't a draft, and it wasn't my imagination, and it wasn't Ken playing stupid tricks again. Go in there yourself if you think I'm kidding."

At that very moment, Producer Dave felt something cold too. The cold seemed to come from the stage, but nothing was up there but the curtains. Seeing the curtains closed bothered him, though, for some reason. He thought he'd have the crew open them after they finally got the intro in the can.

Hey—they could shoot it as though the curtains were opening all by themselves. Good one!

Reassured, he patted Karla on the back reassuringly. "It's OK. We're all right here, you know. If the boogeyman wants to get you, he's gonna have to go through us."

She grimaced; he backtracked. "But he's *not* gonna get you. It's just a show, OK? Just a dumb TV show. So go get yourself some popcorn. Take a few minutes."

Karla nodded. She moved slowly toward the center aisle, almost sleepwalking, seemingly lost in thought. Then she turned to face the house and shouted, *"Weasel shit!"*

(Backstage, Late Annabelle flinched. "We have weasels?")

The crew leaped out of their seats to give her a standing ovation. She ignored it, flopping angrily into a seat on the opposite aisle. Sensing a need for more damage control, Producer Dave joined her.

So it was that the whole *Ghost Town* company was seated and facing the stage when the main feature started.

Late Show

THE MAIN FEATURE started with a scream. It was one of those shrill, arcing screams that make human hair stand on end—the one Late Mabel had always wanted to use in her Juliet-in-the-tomb scene, but those Philistine directors always told her it was too stagy. What did *they* know?

"What was that?" Ken asked, uneasy. "I thought I heard a—"

Upstage, Late Midge screamed louder (and, she knew, better). As written, Lady Macbeth was more screamee than screamer, but the evening was already off-book, and besides, theatrical screaming was fun. Not to mention that she'd had better reviews for Juliet than that stage hog Mabel ever did.

Karla edged closer to Producer Dave, hoping he would tell her something good.

"Relax," he told her. "It's got to be the wind. It's a windy—"

At which point the Wurlitzer came to life, all its lights flashing as it raised itself over the stage. The tune was "Chopsticks," and the triple keyboards were playing themselves.

The *Ghost Town* personnel were 115 percent sober now and frozen to their seats. Unnoticed by any of them, the cameras floated into the air and started rolling, ostensibly recording an empty stage and a playing organ that no one was playing. At the same time, the ghost-hunter equipment started "working." The tinny travel alarm on the ectoplasm sensor went off. The super-EVP voice recorder played back scary sounds (dragging chains, creaking floorboards, eerie *Ooooooooo*s). The ultrasensitive multiplane night-vision image recorder clicked off a few Polaroids, evidently of nothing.

The next bad things were a flash-bang and a cloud of theatrical smoke, which cleared to reveal a transparent Phantom of the Opera at the organ. The crashes around the building were all the exit doors slamming and locking.

Karla screamed. So did Producer Dave's production assistant. So did the men. Then it got worse.

As the organ descended to picture position, the Phantom banged out the terrifying opening bars of Bach's Toccata and Fugue in D minor (not that the music mattered, because the 1925 Lon Chaney film was silent, but who does *Phantom* without the Toccata and Fugue?). In the instant that the mortals recognized the scary music, they knew the puffs of white smoke popping out of the organ pipes for what they were: the disembodied heads of ghost children, mouths opening and closing in time with the notes they appeared to be singing.

("Nice entrance, Pinky!" Late Elsie/Ophelia, already dripping wet, called from her post at the edge of the stage. He winked at her but kept playing.)

The stage curtains opened—by themselves—and the footlights came up on the ghosts. Transparent though they were to mortal eyes, the mortals saw them clearly. There was no time to faint before the Alhambra exploded in a glorious orgy of horror, flamboyance, and excess:

> • Both Macbeths and the witches howled and keened as they whirled in a vicious circle upstage. It was completely unscripted but Felt Right. Late Midge got so caught up in the thing that she almost mowed down Late Robert . . .
>
> • . . . who was declaiming downstage left as Oedipus Rex, bloody rubber eyeballs dangling on strings from the eyeholes of his mask—a proper Greek theater mask, he wanted them all to know. He'd been classically trained.
>
> • Late Harold gave them Alas Poor Yorick, which might have been scary enough except that the skull was Late Arnie's head and he still had the hat on. ("You're supposed to be a skull!" Late Harold whispered furiously. "Improvise!" Late Arnie hissed back.)
>
> • At the Wurlitzer end of downstage, Late Lil, portraying the It Girl, competed shamelessly for audience attention with some of the flappers and Sennett girls, Late Elsie's Ophelia (still dripping), and Late Walter's Julius Caesar. Caesar kept hiking up his toga to flash a leg, an effect ruined only slightly by all the prop knives in his chest and all the fake blood.
>
> • Everywhere else, from balcony to catwalk, ghost extras committed savage acts of theater.

High above the house, Matilda the Ex-Theater Cat lay curled in the middle of the chandelier, waiting for her cue. She didn't have long to wait. When Late Pinky veered from Bach to *Carmina Burana*, Matilda swung the chandelier.

At which point all the theater's exit doors slammed open again.

That one did it. The humans dropped their popcorn, wet their collective pants, and ran screaming into the night.

Aftershow

THE ALHAMBRA PLAYERS celebrated with the champagne they'd nicked from one of the bricked-up storerooms that the new owners hadn't found yet. Late Marvin thought the bottles were left over from some cast party decades ago; they were dusty enough and a cheap-enough brand to be just what the old owner would buy. "What was his name?" he asked. "The young guy who owned this place in the Twenties. Porter, wasn't it?"

"It was Porter," Late Mabel confirmed. "Phineas Aloysius Porter. He had the most beautiful eyes, for a man. Beautiful hands, too. Magnificent ass. He's been dead and gone on for years." She raised her glass to the heavens (or the balcony) in salute, drained it, and held it out to a ghost extra for refilling. "I slept with him, you know."

Late Lil shrugged. "So did I."

"So did I," Late Midge said.

"Me too," said Late Pinky. "What of it?"

The ghosts goggled at him in varying degrees of disbelief.

"You did not," Late Annabelle accused.

Laughing, Late Pinky pulled off his Phantom mask. "I did not. Just wanted to see your face when I said it, Annie."

Late Annabelle was in an aftershow mood, though, so she kept after him. "You had an awful lot of fun playing that *organ* tonight. *If* you get my drift."

Most of the other ghosts booed and threw the TV crew's popcorn at her. Late Robert took a higher road, as befitted a classically trained artist. "Pinky was very good, you know," he told her. "And that thing with the baby heads was such a nice touch."

"Woof!" Late Walter agreed. "That almost scared *me.*"

"I propose a toast," said Late Harold, raising his glass. "To Pinky."

They drank to him.

"To a good night's work well done," Late Lil suggested.

They drank to that.

"To Finney Porter's ass," said Late Walter.

They drank to it.

"Gosh, that was fun," Late Midge said, already wistful. "Best fun in years. We should do it again."

A mortal stepped out of the shadows below the balcony. "Want to?" Mr. Griffith asked.

The ghosts shrieked in terrified surprise.

Three Months Later

THE ALHAMBRA ENJOYED great success with its new Friday Frights series. Mr. Griffith and the other owners were happy. The ghosts were happy too. Improvising was way more fun than memorizing lines and following some bonehead director's blocking—unless you were one of the Stratford-on-Avon snobs, but you could improvise Shakespeare too. Late Marvin tried it and got rave reviews for playing Hamlet as Count Orlok from *Nosferatu*. (A vampire Hamlet made a certain sort of sense when you thought about it.)

Ghost Town had a less-happy ending. The day after the unfinished Alhambra taping, Producer Dave sent the crew back for the equipment, most of which cost too much to leave behind. Stone-faced, Karla's sister-in-law let them into the theater; shamefaced, they grabbed the gear and beat it.

Later that day, back at the station, Producer Dave ran the raw camera footage to see what could be repurposed; he still owed WDIM an episode. What he saw confused and startled and frightened him, even in broad daylight. He twisted an ankle sprinting to the station manager's office with the footage.

The station manager canceled *Ghost Town* on the spot. She said she'd never seen such cheesy special effects.

THIS CONCLUDES
OUR BROADCAST DAY

IF YOU WERE a kid in the I City area in the 1950s, you knew three things for sure: There were more of you than anyone else, candy-coated cereal was part of a complete breakfast, and WVTV was the best TV station ever. You and your friends might argue the fourth (Yankees or Giants, Elvis or Buddy Holly, Godzilla or King Kong), but there was no question about the third. WVTV was your Hollywood.

It wasn't much of a station, really, even by small-city standards. Sam Tarzes, who owned a radio-manufacturing plant and a couple of radio stations, built it on a shoestring in 1949 to see what would happen with this newfangled television thing. The station still ran on a shoestring. Tarzes preferred radio. "What's so great about television?" he liked to ask. "It's radio with pictures."

And so it was until the interns came.

Getting mixed up with the college hadn't been Tarzes's idea. The school's new broadcasting department wanted to send interns to work at WVTV in the summers—again, not his idea. But it turned out that interns worked cheap. It also turned out that some of them fooled around with the theater department and could act a little when they had to. He put them to work recording promos and low-budget local commercials for free. The day an intern decided to wear a cowboy hat for a car spot was the day the light bulb went on over Tarzes's head.

The following week, *Tumbleweed Theater* premiered—fifteen minutes one Friday afternoon between Coronet films and cartoons. The phone lines lit up. WVTV never looked back.

If you were a kid in the I City area in the late 1950s, you watched all these shows religiously every weekday afternoon from three to five:

> *Cartoon Carnival:* Clarence the Clown's program was the
> only WVTV show with a live studio audience. Like all clowns,

Clarence told silly jokes, honked a bicycle horn, and squirted seltzer between cartoons. The cartoons were good, though—mostly old Merrie Melodies. If you were lucky, Clarence might show an early Bugs Bunny.

Miss Priscilla's Tea Party: Yes, boys watched Miss Priscilla too. If you were a boy, you tuned in to make fun of her tiara and call her Miss Priss to upset your sister, but you tuned in all the same. Miss Priscilla was the most glamorous lady you'd ever seen, even in the movies, and though you couldn't tell (on your black-and-white TV) what color her pretty dress was, you knew it was pink. She poured tea every weekday afternoon at 3:30, served little cakes (you knew they were pink), and sang and played her accordion between cartoons.

Zoo and You: The kids watched this show mainly because it was on. But the animals could be sort of interesting sometimes, and Jungle Jim looked important in his safari clothes, with that funny hat. (When the boys found out that the hat was called a pith helmet, they peed themselves laughing.) The I City Zoo's small collection limited program variety; more often than not, Jungle Jim did his show from the reptile house. That was fine with his pint-size viewers, though, because it got the boys even with the girls for having to watch Miss Priss first.

Tumbleweed Theater: The 'Weed was the Big Kahuna of WVTV productions, the best-loved of them all. Cowboy Joe's hat, bandanna, and guitar were as iconic to modern kids as FDR's cigarette holder was to their parents, and every small viewer wanted a Sagebrush. Sagebrush was Cowboy Joe's horse. The big Appaloosa never got into the studio (Tarzes was a clean freak, and a horse was a horse), appearing only in pretaped segments. Not that it mattered to the kids. A horse was a horse, on set or not, and this one was Cowboy Joe's best friend.

Late on Fridays, you also watched this:

Cemetery Cinema with Doug and Lonesome Graves: Doug Graves was the host. Lonesome was his dog. His *ghost* dog. Lonesome was more lupine than canine—a huge gray-and-white beast with one blue eye and one white one, due to heterochromia iridum—but very well trained. (See above about Tarzes and animals in studio.) The show ran every Friday from 11:30 p.m. to 1 a.m., way past bedtime, but every child in the WVTV viewing area watched it, usually behind their parents' backs.

The movies themselves weren't so frightening—mostly Z-grade foreign horror flicks with unsynchronized dubbing— but the hosts gave the kids the creeps. Doug had that long black coat, that dirty shovel, and those horrible pointy fangs, and Lonesome looked enough like a ghost dog to be convincingly spectral. At least once every show, Doug got Lonesome to howl, and it was hide-under-your-blankie scary even when you knew it was coming.

They were only five shows, but they made buckets of money for Tarzes. Most of the college kids stayed on—and worked for peanuts—after graduation. Production costs (and values) were low. Most of the cartoons and movies that filled out the programs cost little to acquire. Yet advertisers bought time on those shows like time was going out of style. There were more kids than anyone else in the WVTV viewing area, and you could never go wrong playing to kids in the Fifties.

Everything was fine, dandy, and normal as apple pie with vanilla ice cream until Cowboy Joe went mad.

NOBODY KNEW AT first that Cowboy Joe was mad. He came to work on a Tuesday with the sniffles ("Horse fever," he told his young viewers on the air that afternoon) and missed work on Wednesday, so Tarzes sent him to Doc Driver in Normburg on Thursday.

No one knew then that Doc Driver was mad too. Only his nurse knew about the experiments in the basement, and she wasn't telling.

On the appointed morning, Cowboy Joe showed up at Doc's office in street clothes, without his guitar, and under his real name (Buddy Miller). Doc knew him, though. Doc had spent tens of dollars on Cowboy Joe merchandise for his sons and had heard the *Tumbleweed Theater* theme song too many times. He hated Cowboy Joe now. So when the hated cowpoke came in with a mild upper respiratory infection, Doc knew what to do.

"Take two of these every night," the doctor said, handing him a small white cardboard box full of pills, "and see how you feel in a week."

The pills came from a large brown glass bottle in Doc's pharmacy cabinet, a bottle with a MegaPharma Labs label identifying the compound as extra-long-lasting benzofluoxazine salts. Also on the label was the large red word EXPERIMENTAL. For good measure, Doc sprayed the pillbox with something he'd been distilling in the basement—a mixture of fluoride and municipal tap water. Then he sat back to see what would happen.

What happened was that Cowboy Joe went to bed Thursday night as Buddy Miller, ordinary young American man with the sniffles, and woke up Friday morning as Cowboy Joe for real.

He felt great. Completely cured! He went to work early.

To share the wealth with his friends and give them a good day too, he dumped the rest of Doc Driver's pills into the dressing-room percolator.

THE FIRST SIGN of trouble came as soon as possible: minutes before *Cartoon Carnival* went on the air that day. Clarence the Clown was in fact a mild-mannered WVTV sales rep named Milton Sweet who did the show for extra income, and he'd always been fond of children, having several of his own and a couple of grandbabies. When he appeared on set that Friday, though, his painted smile seemed strained and fake, even hostile. He ignored the excited children in the studio audience and lit a real, nonexploding cigar in full view of them.

"No smoking in front of the kids, Miltie," the camera operator said.

The junior assistant director tried to fan the fumes away with a cue card. "Gosh-darn it, Miltie, that thing stinks. Take it outside."

"Get it off the set, buddy," the head grip growled.

Expressionless under his painted smile, the clown squirted the three adults with seltzer. The children loved it. Then he squirted the children, who continued to love it.

But the junior assistant director saw the cold glitter in the clown's eye as he stalked off-set. He'd always liked clowns, but now he thought he understood why some people didn't.

THE CIGAR INCIDENT was the first of many during that day's *Carnival*. Clarence refused to answer to "Miltie" when addressed as such.

He made sarcastic remarks about the cartoons while they played on the studio monitor. He kicked a production assistant for trying to straighten his curly red clown wig, which had gone awry when he tried to throttle the cue-card boy.

The last straw came during a Bugs Bunny–Elmer Fudd cartoon when Clarence stalked off to the dressing room and came back with a rifle. A short, vicious scuffle for the weapon ensued. The crew won. The head grip sat on Clarence's head while someone ran to get Mr. Tarzes.

The children, of course, were connoisseurs of cartoon violence (which this was) and shrieked their approval even while their horrified mothers bundled them off the set.

"Go home and sleep it off, Miltie," the junior assistant director told him. What the clown told him back really can't be repeated.

Nothing got better after that. Miss Priscilla threw an offscreen tantrum right before the tea party because a few sequins on her taffeta dress were coming unglued. She refused to play "Lady of Spain" one more time on her #*^&@$! accordion; she insisted on trying to work out how to play "Great Balls of Fire" instead. Tarzes's secretary had to threaten her with contract papers to get her to behave, but it was a near thing: Priscilla flew the twin birds at her a split-second before the ON AIR sign lit again.

At the zoo, Jungle Jim behaved oddly too. Even the snakes were avoiding him. In one segment, he spoke of the sorrow of life in captivity and offered to feed a keeper to the crocodile for payback. In the next, he waved a big stick around and offered to kill every living creature in the zoo to show them who was boss. The head zookeeper took him aside after the show and told him to come back in a better mood Monday or not at all.

Which left the *Weed.* Cowboy Joe carried on with that day's show pretty much as usual—singing, introducing cartoons, telling corny Western jokes—until it came time for one of the pretaped segments with Sagebrush. Sagebrush was in fact Tessie, a gentle mare who lived at Bar Nunn Stables and who had great patience with Cowboy Joe's antics, which included putting a cowboy hat on her and pretend-riding her while fake-playing guitar. The pretaped segment that day was more of the same. Tessie blinked politely through it and graciously accepted the carrots that Cowboy Joe's producer gave her afterward. Being a horse, she'd done something equine immediately after that, and Cowboy Joe went down in it, being a step too slow.

Everyone laughed at the time, even Joe. But if he'd forgiven his co-star, he hadn't forgotten. As soon as the prerecorded stable segment was over that day, he looked straight into the camera and told the kids he was leaving I City to go West and punch some cows—and he might punch Sagebrush too because he was really a girl named Tessie.

The show had ten minutes left to run that afternoon. The director ordered more cartoons to fill the rest of Cowboy Joe's airtime, handed his headset and clipboard to his assistant, and punched Cowboy Joe.

SAM TARZES CALLED a production meeting at 5:01 p.m. The unruly hosts straggled in unwillingly, still wearing their costumes and makeup. (Cowboy Joe was using his bandanna to mop his nose, which was still bleeding.) They listened unwillingly to what Tarzes had to say, which reduced to this: Straighten up and fly right.

When the meeting was over, the hosts walked to the parking lot as a group. No one said a word until Clarence the Clown announced that he hated all their guts and the others told him that they hated his back.

In passing, they passed Doug Graves, who was on his way in. They told him they hated his guts too.

Doug shrugged. He had a few bits to prerecord for that night's *Cemetery Cinema* and a date with a pretty girl intern later, so their hate rolled off him.

Also, they'd left him some coffee in the dressing room, for once, so how mad could they be? He emptied the percolator into a big mug and drank it all down.

SAM TARZES CALLED another production meeting for first thing Monday morning. Doug Graves was front and center at this one, having beheaded a rat with his shovel on-air Friday night—a *real* rat—and then sicced Lonesome on the cameraman. (Fortunately, the dog had been more interested in the rat.)

Tarzes regarded his hosts in frosty silence. They'd all reported in full costume and makeup—even Doug, who didn't have a show that night but showed up camera-ready, in the long black coat and the fake fangs, carrying the dirty shovel as always. When Tarzes asked why, he said he'd just left Lonesome in the cemetery. Then he laughed maniacally.

Miss Priscilla, who was sitting next to him, got up and changed chairs.

A quick word with his secretary and a short phone call later, Tarzes told Doug to stop making up stories. Lonesome was at home with his owners, happy and healthy, eating Ken-L Ration. "No one's dead, Mr. Graves," he concluded.

The host smiled evilly. "Wait."

Jungle Jim, who'd been sitting on Doug's other side, also got up and moved. He was careful how he handled the pith helmet, which had a live snake curled up inside, but nobody needed to know.

Clarence the Clown and Cowboy Joe, however, merely seemed bored. Clarence was leaning back insolently in his chair, his big clown shoes propped on the table, smoking a fat real cigar, and Cowboy Joe kept playing with a toy six-shooter—spinning the barrel, squeezing off "shots," blowing "smoke" off the muzzle, spinning the barrel. The small noises were getting on Tarzes's nerves.

"I don't know what's gotten into all you jokers," the boss said, "but it stops now. *Today*. Anybody puts a toe over the line today gets a pink slip. You get me?"

For answer, Miss Priscilla gave him a venomous smile, sweet as candied tarantula, and played the *Looney Tunes* theme* on her accordion. It wasn't much of an answer, but it was close enough.

BY FRIDAY, CIVILIZATION still held at WVTV, but barely. All the children's hosts were living their characters day and night, making the crews, interns, and office workers unhappy. Cowboy Joe had tried to ride a stenographer who'd bent down to pick up a pencil he'd dropped on purpose, and Tarzes was threatening pink slips again.

("Wasn't gonna use the spurs, you big baby," Cowboy Joe snarled at her as they left the boss's office. Clarence the Clown, who'd been waiting in the hall, merely gave her a hateful look.)

Still, the show had to go on. All five shows that day, in fact. Since Wednesday, when Miss Priscilla had been caught in a broom closet blowing one of the handsomer interns, Tarzes had extra security guards posted all over the station. Everything was locked down, and the sets were locked tightest of all. You couldn't get anywhere near a set without a pass, not even if you worked in the building. As an extra precaution, there was no studio audience for *Cartoon Carnival* that day. The kiddies and moms who had tickets got vouchers for future shows and were sent home with autographed photos of the famous clown.

"The Merry-Go-Round Broke Down" (1937; Cliff Friend and Dave Franklin)

As for Jungle Jim, he was on a timeout from the zoo, having pelted the chimps with banana peels on Thursday. He'd be doing his Friday program from the sales manager's office, talking about the sales manager's tropical fish. (They were small fish in a large bowl but would look ten pounds heavier on TV.) To ensure that nothing funny would happen, two security guards were deployed to guard the fish.

It was 2:50 p.m.

AT 5:05, TARZES drove home for dinner. His daytime kiddie stars would have dinner in jail if they got processed in time. Most of the sets were smoldering ruins; the station manager's fishbowl was broken; the fish were in a better world; several security guards had quit; the director was still picking pieces of Miss Priscilla's accordion out of his hair.

"You should sell that station, Sammy," his wife told him, not for the first time. "You don't need the money, and who needs the grief?"

Morosely, Tarzes toyed with his goulash. He didn't need the money, that was true, but he liked TV all right now. Though he would never have told his wife, he liked Miss Priscilla all right too. Mamie didn't need *that* grief.

Besides, the girl of his moderately filthy dreams was locked up downtown, where he couldn't get to her. Someone else could, though. The brawny sergeant who'd carried her to the paddy wagon was exactly her type, and Tarzes saw the look that had passed between them when he frisked her. He just knew she was blowing the big cop in the broom closet at the jail at that very moment.

(In fact, Sergeant Moller had suggested the laundry room.)

"I think I'll go back tonight for the Graves show," Tarzes said. "Keep an eye on things."

Mamie paused in the process of spooning more peas onto his plate. "Don't you have police there for that?"

"I don't trust the police."

"Since when?"

Tarzes ate his second helping of peas in silence. He finished his goulash and fruit cup, chased them with angel food cake with pink icing, drank two more cups of A&P's best without saying a word.

For her part, Mamie had an extra slice of cake. She knew about Miss Priscilla. She only hoped that the cop her husband didn't trust would give that hussy the clap.

"ALL QUIET, MR. Tarzes," the night station manager reported.

Tarzes nodded and went straight to Studio B. The extra security guards were milling around looking bored, but they were there, at least. So were a few sheriff's deputies. Technically, the WVTV property was inside city limits, but only just inside them (corn grew half a mile down Trench Road), and the sheriff played golf with Tarzes sometimes. Sending a few men over to the station was both a favor and a way to find out exactly what had happened earlier that day. (Police Chief Marlowe wasn't talking.)

Stagehands were heaving the back wall of the set into place when Tarzes arrived. Airtime was half an hour away; he reminded them that they were cutting it close.

"We had some trouble with the coffin, Mr. Tarzes," the stage manager explained. "It didn't want to open."

"It's only plywood."

"Sure it is. The hinges got rusty, that's all. We put on new ones in the end."

Tarzes glanced at the prop coffin, standing upright in its usual place. Doug Graves opened it at the start of each show; the plastic skeleton inside danced whenever the host told a joke. Sometimes, a stagehand pulled the skeleton's strings too hard and broke a few, but that was all part of the fun.

"Make sure those strings don't show on camera tonight," he said.

"Yes, Mr. Tarzes."

He turned to the night manager. "Talent ready?"

The night manager assured him that they were. Doug was in his dressing room, smoking a preshow cigarette; the dog's owner was taking Lonesome for one last preshow walk.

"I don't want trouble tonight, George."

"No, Mr. Tarzes," the night manager said.

The station owner dismissed him with a nod. Then he inspected the snack table. Someone had brought in a box of glazed yeast doughnuts from Hap's Bakery two counties over. Tarzes put a couple of the sticky things on a napkin and ate them standing up, watching the crew finish dressing and lighting the set.

AT THE STROKE of 11:30, the prerecorded theme played in Studio B, less music than howling, screeching, and flapping. The stagehands turned on the big fans to blow the dry-ice fumes onto the set, and on cue, a tall man in a long black coat with a shovel over his shoulder stepped out of the fog into the stage lights. A large, weird-eyed Siberian husky followed.

"Welllllllcome," Doug Graves said to camera in his deepest, most sepulchral voice. Then he smiled that pointy smile.

Across the viewing area, children who were supposed to be in bed hid under pillows and furniture. Adults laughed indulgently. On set, the director cued Doug to open the coffin. Next to the cameraman, a production assistant held up the cue card: GOOD EVENING, BORIS. [WAIT WAIT WAIT] WORM GOT YOUR TONGUE?

Tarzes sipped more bitter stage coffee from his paper cup and counted the law-enforcement personnel again.

Three seconds passed. Six seconds. Ten. Doug continued to stand on his mark without saying his lines, smiling and staring into the camera, the business end of the shovel parked over his right shoulder.

"Open the box, Doug!" the director stage-whispered urgently.

"Do you want me to open the coffin?" Doug replied to camera.

Off camera, crew and security personnel made frantic gestures in the affirmative.

"Lonesome, should I open the coffin?"

The dog gazed up at him placidly. He'd just had several treats, and he knew there were more in the man's pockets, so he was content to go along with whatever the man wanted.

By now, the director was turning cardiac red, and only a quick-thinking stagehand kept him from charging the talent. While everyone watched the two men struggle, a few uninvited guests entered the studio and quietly took up positions behind the crew.

"I think I'll open the coffin," Doug said. "Come, Lonesome. Let's see who's in it tonight."

Tarzes, standing to the left of the camera, was surprised to find himself in doubt. Not twenty minutes before, he'd watched the crew double-check the strings on the plastic skeleton and then close the lid of the fake coffin. No one had gone near it since except the stagehand who worked the strings, and that was only for a test.

Everyone watched Doug cross the set and approach the plywood coffin. Everyone watched him shift the dirty shovel to his left hand. He cheated to the camera while he reached for the coffin handle with his right hand, and everyone saw him open the lid.

The lid moved smoothly on its brand-new hinges but squeaked like a rusty gate. Something flew out of the coffin before the lid was fully open. Then another thing. Then more of them.

Bats.

Someone screamed.

"Cut!" the director shouted. "*Cut*, God damn you, cut!"

Screens all over the viewing area went black a split-second later, but not before the skeleton—a real skeleton, freshly dug up from a real graveyard—stepped out of the fake coffin.

Frozen in horror, crew, security, and Tarzes never saw Cowboy Joe, Clarence the Clown, Miss Priscilla, and Jungle Jim coming up from behind.

THE PAPERS WOULD call it the I City Massacre, even though WVTV was only technically inside city limits. Media came from all over the country, even *Life* and *Look* magazines. You couldn't keep a story like that local, and it *was* a massacre. But who had massacred whom, no one could say. There was no one to question, much less arrest. No one survived but the dog.

The dog *was* very well trained, though. He'd eaten only part of only one security guard, and the guard *had* been trying to club him with a heavy flashlight at the time. Self-defense, the special judge ruled.

The grave-robbed skeleton was reinterred with honors and sincerest apologies to the family. Mamie Tarzes paid for everything. There were rumors that King's Hill Cemetery had given her a volume discount, given the number of burials involved.

There were rumors, too, that Doug Graves had beheaded Tarzes with a shovel before the sheriff's department arrived, but with the studio being on fire like that, it was hard to tell what had happened where, or when, or to whom. When the fire was finally out and the smoke began to clear, the searchers found only bits and pieces in the rubble: Cowboy Joe's harmonica, Clarence the Clown's red-ball nose, half the director's headset, and a single pink feather from Miss Priscilla's boa.

Sergeant Moller was put on administrative leave for letting the TV hosts out of jail. What Miss Priscilla had posted as bail was nonnegotiable in trade, and the laundry room had needed a good scouring afterward.

In time, investigators connected the dots to Cowboy Joe's visit to Doc Driver. But the good doctor was never charged with anything. As he told them, the side effects of medications are unpredictable. He also said he'd never liked that expletive Cowboy Joe anyway.

Quietly, the Widow Tarzes sold her interest in what had been WVTV to a local manufacturer of television sets. The factory owner changed the call letters and started over. There'd be no more killer clowns or homicidal cowboys, but he figured that the rest of the kiddie shows would be fine after recasting.

They were. In fact, the new station prospered far more than the old one had. If you were a kid in the I City area in the 1960s, you knew three things for sure: There were more of you than anyone else, candy-coated cereal was part of a complete breakfast, and WTTT was the best TV station ever.

SWITCH

FOR AS LONG as she could remember, Allie had been a seeker. Literally—her lead archetypes were Wanderer and Magician, which added up to Seeker in most archetypal psychologies, most of which she'd studied in the course of her quest. She'd read psychology in greater depth than many grad students did, and in wider, less-academic realms. She'd chased light and truth over fathomless seas of time, across continents, through discipline after discipline, practice after practice, coming closer to enlightenment all the time. She was as Eastern by then as a Westerner could be.

—In principle, that is. A couple of weeks in India every couple of years were one thing; life without an occasional Chardonnay or bite of luxury chocolate was another. She worried that this made her a hypocrite when in fact it made her human. She knew that most ascetics ended badly, and she had no desire to end badly, even if Maya *was* going to roll up like a movie screen at the end and reveal mortal life to be a slapstick short.

But that was the problem: the end. At heart, every Eastern practice was all, and only, about it. In *her* heart, Allie liked life and didn't want to miss it, not even for showers of blessings in a distant afterworld. She'd struggled with what she saw as her own duplicity and rebellion for years.

Then came the day when she lost her faith—or, rather, had it taken from her.

All she'd done was turn up early for her nine o'clock meditation class, which meant waiting outside the meditation room for the eight o'clock class to let out. This room was a rented space on the ground floor of a busy commercial building, which like most commercial buildings played Muzak in its public spaces. Allie normally ran late to class and had never noticed the Muzak before. But that day, while she waited in the hall, the system played a dumb, catchy, dirty song that she'd loved to dance to in high school.

You can't help what your feet do when you hear certain songs—not if you're human.

Allie was alone, but she remembered how to dance alone. She'd forgotten how much fun dancing was. She was getting all the way into the spirit of the exercise by giving the wall a playful bump (and OK, a tiny grind) when the door of the meditation room opened. Her local guru was first out. He heard all, he saw all, and that was that.

One public lapse in ten years of scrupulous purity, and she was persona non grata in Nirvana—excommunicated, but without a church.

Allie was as close to angry as an Easternized Westerner could be, and *should* have been, but it never occurred to her to feel what she felt, much less express it. There was no obvious source of closure for a seeker who'd been dumped by a guru, which meant she'd have to come up with her own cleansing ritual.

First, she tried forgiveness.

Next, she tried chanting, extra yoga, additional incense, more bells. She lit candles and gazed into crystals. She played her favorite ragas while she swayed and wept and prayed.

Nothing.

Finally, she did what she'd never thought to do before: the opposite.

Allie booked a flight and two nights in a nice hotel in New Orleans. She'd always heard how wicked and depraved New Orleans was. Maybe she'd feel better there by comparison.

ZOEY WAS A witch. Not a bad one, particularly, but a dark one. She'd grown up in upper-class circumstances, hung out at the country club, and followed all the WASPy rules, which was a surefire recipe for rebellion the first chance she got.

Later, she could never quite remember what triggered it. She'd read Vonnegut, Huxley, Orwell, and the like by the carload, with no discernible effect. She'd also read Cayce, Pike, and Crowley, ditto. Her liking for the occult had been constant, so she couldn't point to any one thing that turned her.

It might have been *The Satanic Bible*, with the opening warning/threat that she never forgot. But it was probably the witch band.

This band had no name—only a string of obscure symbols. It had no recording contract—only bootlegs. It was mediocre musically at best. But its members called themselves witches, dressed like Stevie Nicks in her "Rhiannon" period, had it, flaunted it, and were much too cool for school, so Zoey loved them. They were all image, but she bought it hook, line, and sinker, not to mention heart and soul. She wanted to be like that, freak her parents like that.

Eventually, she did. By then, though, the witch band didn't matter. She was all about the Dark.

Where she lived, she was alone in it. There were no classes for makeshift witches at the local Y; there were no Meetups within a three-hour drive. She had just enough sense of humor not to join the regional coven, which operated out of the basement of an occult bookstore in a nearby college town and ran mostly to Goth kids and middle-aged Cure fans who presented like the *Portlandia* Weirdos.

Mostly, she bought supplies and spellbooks over the Internet and cast spells in her apartment. A few worked a little; most didn't at all. She kept trying. The point was that she was rebelling.

That sort of rebellion, however, was mostly insolence, which had no true power. Zoey thought the larger point might *be* power.

Unluckily, there was no dark force to tap in her part of the country. (The red-caps crowd didn't count.) She thought about it and thought about it and finally came up with New Orleans. Voodoo, black magic, big juju. Her parents would hate it. Perfect!

She called a cousin who was still a travel agent and booked a three-day trip to check out the city. The flight had connections, but connection was what she was after.

Connection to what? She meant to find out. It might make her feel better.

THEY MET OVER voodoo. Zoey was in a dark corner of the shop checking out a spell candle when Allie stumbled over a loose floorboard in passing and bumped her. The candle went flying, glass holder and all, into Allie's open bag.

Both of them let out a breath that they didn't know they'd been holding and then laughed simultaneously.

"Sorry," Allie said.

"You're fine," Zoey assured her.

Allie pulled the candle out of her bag, but instead of handing it over straightaway, she read its markings. "What does this mean, 'Black Cat'?"

Zoey lied and said she didn't know; she was only looking.

"Me too. But you might want to look at the blue candles instead. They're more spiritual."

The witch frowned slightly. "Are they?"

"Blue is a healing color. That's what my guru says, anyway. *Said*."

Healing? A guru? Worse and worse. "Maybe now would be a good time to tell you that I'm a witch."

The blonde woman stared at the dark-haired one for a moment. Then she laughed again. "No, you're not."

"Yes, I am. But who has a guru?"

"I do. . . . Well, I *did*. What difference does it make?"

The witch regarded her coolly. "It doesn't. I was only making small talk."

"That was small, all right."

Silence.

"Right, then. If you'll give me back the candle, you can go your own way."

Allie relinquished the Black Cat. "Here you go. It wasn't *really* nice meeting you, I guess, but—"

"Not very, was it? So long."

They smiled tightly and walked in opposite directions. On her way out of the shop, Allie passed a clerk who'd been eavesdropping; to her surprise, he winked at her.

THAT SHOULD HAVE been that, but the Mysteries are strong in New Orleans. That afternoon, Allie took a cemetery tour, hoping for spiritual communion and (with luck) a sign from the Hereafter. The tour guide had stopped her group next to Marie Laveau's tomb and was pointing out its features when another tour group stopped on the opposite side. The woman in black from the voodoo shop was at the front of that group, wearing oddly incongruous sunglasses and a faint smile that verged on a smirk.

They saw each other at the same time. Frowning, Allie pulled down her own sunglasses to verify. Zoey didn't quite manage not to curse. Everyone noticed.

Luckily, the tour guides started talking much louder then, jockeying for position and supremacy, which drew most of their customers' attention back. After a minute or two of that, everyone wanted the guides to shut up and just punch each other, already. It was too hot for a fight but also too hot to stand in the broiling sun doing nothing, and the tourists were getting restless. So was the witch, who was beginning to repent wearing black; a couple of the purple streaks in her dark hair were starting to drip.

Allie ostentatiously fanned herself with her sari-style top (pastel, lightweight, pretty). When Zoey looked over, she uncapped her water bottle and took an extra-long drink.

In nuclear silence, Zoey cast the only voodoo curse she knew. Pity that the woman's head stayed on.

The witch turned her back for the rest of the time her tour group was at the Laveau tomb. This pleased Allie, who for once felt no guilt about being pleased.

But she didn't understand why some of the men in her tour group smiled at her that way.

NEITHER, AT DINNERTIME, did she understand how she ended up sitting at a long zinc bar in a repurposed streetcar next to the witch.

The concierge at Allie's hotel had recommended the restaurant, which was why she was there at all. As for Zoey, she'd been aimlessly riding a St. Charles streetcar when she saw it, realized that she was hungry, and pulled the bell cord to get off. The establishment was jammed to capacity and as loud as ten frat houses on twenty Saturday nights (it was essentially a tin can), but whatever was cooking smelled well worth the bother of sitting at the bar. She ordered a bitters and inhaled the spicy, fatty, delicious air with pleasure while reading the menu on the chalkboard. She paid no attention when someone slid into the seat to her right—the only one left in the house. Only when that someone drew a sharp breath did she look over.

"Really?" Zoey asked, pained.

Allie closed her eyes and recited a mantra until she was calm enough to answer. But all she did then was smile what she hoped was a maddening smile.

It *did* madden the witch a little. "Great. This is exactly what I need right now: New Age Barbie."

Which in turn made Allie mad. "Oh, get off your broom, *Hocus Pocus*. Can't we pretend to be civilized just this once?"

"Can't we pretend we don't know each other?"

"We *don't* know each other."

"Then it'll be easy, won't it?" Zoey waved again to get the bartender's attention; he'd been too busy ogling Allie to notice the first time. "Shrimp po-boy, please. With cyanide."

Allie tried not to smile a little, failed, and said she'd have the same.

Realizing now that hitting on the blonde babe would be pointless, the bartender took the orders and resigned himself to watching what he hoped would happen.

NOT MUCH HAPPENED for a while. Obedient to Zoey's request, Allie had been a perfect stranger throughout dinner, reading a paperback with a Shambhala logo, which Zoey recognized only because a college friend had owned lots of the company's books. (One of her first acts of witchery had been to smuggle a few out of the friend's room and make a bonfire of them behind the administration building.) Even if she'd wanted to talk, the bar end of the streetcar was too noisy; Zoey dimly realized that music had been playing at high volume the whole time, but it was hard to hear under the clamor of undergrad revelry. So she occupied herself instead with dinner and thinking.

Finally, plate clean and glass empty, she asked the bartender for the check. He waved her off. Annoyed, she asked again. Same result. The third time, he told her: The blonde babe had paid both checks before she left.

Dammit. When had she left? "Why would she do that?"

"I dunno," he said, "but if you hurry, you could catch her."

Looking where the bartender pointed, Zoey saw the back of her moving through the garden toward the streetcar stop. Quickly, she felt in her billfold for a tip (a $10 bill, not the $5 she thought) and dropped it on the bar. Then she pushed, shoved, and squeezed her way through the indoor crowd to the outdoor one and through that crowd to the garden—a hard, painful exercise on such a hot night.

She caught up with the woman in the shadow of a live oak between the string lights and the streetlights. The same raucous music that played inside the restaurant also played outside, but not quite as loud.

"Listen," Zoey said, breathing a little hard from the exertion, "you didn't have to do that. Let me pay you back."

"No. Please don't. It's my spiritual discipline for the day."

"Buying dinner for someone you don't like is spiritual discipline?"

"I didn't say I don't like you. You don't like me."

Zoey exhaled sharply in frustration. "I never said that. But you don't like me either."

"Do I have to?"

"No. What*ever*. Why don't we leave it at that? I'll thank you for dinner and leave *that* too. So long again."

"So long again," Allie echoed.

But no one left. They persisted in standing under the live oak, two or three steps outside the string-lighted garden, while a feeling they'd both had all day grew exponentially stronger.

Well, then, to hell with small talk.

"You say you're a witch," Allie said abruptly.

"Yes."

"Black or white?"

"Black."

"Why?"

Zoey considered. A lying wisecrack was on the tip of her tongue, but for some reason, she decided to tell the truth. "Because I don't believe in God."

"Why not?"

"Because I don't have to. Because I hated my parents. What about you? Why are *you* this floral-print hippie chick?"

Allie (who in fact was wearing Laura Ashley, as Zoey knew perfectly well) didn't hesitate. "Because I hated my parents."

The witch made a tiny mock bow. "Your point. But it's still my serve. Do you believe in God?"

"Yes. Of course."

"Prove it."

"Here? Now?"

"Why not? If God is everywhere, why wouldn't God be here? Now?"

"Stop answering questions with questions," Allie demanded. "I *hate* that. Why don't *you* believe?"

Zoey doubled over with laughter, which annoyed her even more. So she'd answered a question with a question herself. So what?

"I'm serious. *Listen.* You say you're a witch. I'm a seeker. But I think we may be the same. You're running the opposite way from me. But the world is round. If we run away from each other long enough, don't you think we'll eventually meet?"

The witch chewed on that idea a little. She'd had the same thought herself: that extremes always meet somewhere. But she normally thought it in context of politics, in which it was normally true. This, though . . .

"What are you doing in New Orleans?" Zoey asked.

"Don't make me ask you the same thing. I mean it."

"All right, then—we'll say it together. Count of three?"

They counted three. Then they said it together. Zoey said, "Looking for the dark," and Allie said, "Looking for the light."

"Oh, for Lucifer's sake," Zoey growled.

"Why? They're the same."

"Since when are New Agers dualists?"

"Since when are witches rationalists?" Allie shot back.

"What's the point in being a seeker if you're not a finder? Where's God in that?"

"Why be a witch if you never get what you want? Where's the Devil?"

Once again, they fell silent. Zoey thought people were starting to stare at them, but she was too intent now on fixing this woman's little floral-print wagon to care.

"Prove it," Zoey said again.

"Prove what?"

"Defend your thesis. Show your work. Prove to me why God and the Devil exist—if they do—and why you think they're the same thing."

"I never said—"

"You said, and I quote you exactly, 'They're the same.'"

"I did. They are. I mean I never said *separation* exists."

Zoey smiled a razor-thin smile. "Of course it does. They go by two names. Do you know your Kipling? 'East is East, and West is West, and never the twain shall meet.' God must be the East, because I know for a *fact* that the Devil is the West. Prove me wrong."

Allie drew herself up tall and met the witch's eyes straight on. "Prove me right."

Silence fell on the garden. Neither woman knew that both of them had been glowing faintly for the past few minutes; the restaurant's patrons couldn't help but notice. But when they stopped talking again, the instant their eyes met and locked, the glow became a burn and the burn became a blaze, and absolutely everyone on the street saw.

All conversation ended. Even the music stopped. But the two women paid no attention. They were locked in a silent duel, blonde and blue-eyed, dark-haired and dark-eyed, dressed in pastels and dressed in black, opposites and antagonists and (who knew?) partners in some higher dimension, staring each other down in deadly earnest for no reason that anyone in the garden could see.

The night manager was about to order the music turned back on when it happened. Allie and Zoey, who didn't even know each other's names, who'd just that instant finished morphing into two bright and unwavering columns of light, suddenly merged into one.

You could read a phone book blocks away by that light. You could see that tiny spark of fire in the dark garden from the Moon.

The spell lasted fully three minutes. None of the watchers dared to move. Only when the columns divided again did the fire begin to dim, and only when it was no brighter than the string lights did Zoey and Allie re-emerge from it.

"Holy shit," someone said—but strangely reverently.

That was one way to put it, Zoey thought. There was another way too. "I think I lost my hat," she told Allie. "We *did* end up miles from here."

Allie smiled. What had happened between them was what she'd been trying to tell the witch—and herself—all along.

"It's all energy," she said. "The trick is how you use it."

THAT WAS THE second night of their stay in New Orleans. On the third day, they toured the cathedral and the voodoo museum—not together. Then they caught their separate flights to their separate homes.

Allie found a new guru in the new city where she moved three months later. As it happened, Zoey had already moved to the same city; she'd found a more-or-less real coven there. They had each other's number but never called. They didn't have to. Some lights, once switched on, stay lit.

Ever after, Allie embraced her dark side, and Zoey did the same with the light. The seeker enjoyed everyday human indulgences (the Talmud says we'll be called to account for the permitted pleasures we failed to enjoy), and the witch opened her heart to Spirit. By these means, both of them finally became enlightened—and much happier.

It may be a small thing, hardly worth mentioning, that Zoey's beloved witch band re-formed soon after as a vaguely Irish New Age group. Their album *White Cat* was playing in Allie's ex-guru's apartment the night he was murdered. It was messy, the police said. Sure looked like voodoo.

SPIRITUS PRANKTI

THE YOUNG COUPLE who'd bought Rectory House had no fear of the stories. That was what everyone said in town, from the real estate agent to the appraiser to the building inspector and the fire marshal. Nobody understood how that could be, though, given the house's reputation. Everybody had a story about it—about headless apparitions, unearthly howls in the night, bloody footprints, pitch-black shadows that shifted shape. Generations of teenagers had visited Rectory House on a dare but never dared to go inside. No one went alone; no one went at midnight.

The house was cursed. The town knew it. No one had tried to live there since the White Murders eighty-seven years ago—ghastly murders with dark hints of occultery. No one had tried to raze the abandoned structure for seventy-eight years, because the last contractor who tried was beheaded by a backhoe, and the backhoe driver said the Devil made him do it.

"You understand that the sale is as-is," the real estate agent told the Duncans on closing day. "You know the building needs work."

Young Mr. Duncan smiled. "Yes, but the building has beautiful bones. We like good bones."

The real estate agent thought, but did not say, that this was fortunate because the back yard was full of bones. The house had in fact been a rectory once, and its back yard was the old churchyard. Whether the bones buried there were good or beautiful, she couldn't say; neither did she care to find out.

"We like the look of it," young Mrs. Duncan assured the real estate agent. "We'll be happy here." She turned to her husband. "Won't we, Mac?"

He put his arm around her and gave her a playful kiss. "I'm already happy, Beth."

As though summoned by the kiss, a cold, inexplicable wind blew through the small room where they stood. There was no window in that room. There was no broken glass anywhere on the property; the county had replaced the damaged panes to keep the birds out. But inexplicable events were only Rectory House being Rectory House.

Trying not to shudder openly, the real estate agent gave her clients a tiny smile. "Shall we sign the papers?"

The couple declined to shake her hand when the deal was done, but that was all right with the agent. All she wanted by then was to get out of that house.

THE DUNCANS MOVED in shortly thereafter. It was early October. The town gossiped that no moving van had been spotted anywhere near the house, that the utilities hadn't been called to turn on the water or lights, that the local grocers hadn't sold Mrs. Duncan so much as an egg. Yet people were living there, plainly enough. Curious townspeople drove by most evenings and saw lights in the windows up on the hill. One who used binoculars also saw furniture and curtains. The furniture was old-fashioned, he said, and the curtains were lace.

"Lace?" the county historian asked, furrowing her brow. "Are you sure?"

The observer shrugged. "It looked like lace. It looked old. There were stains."

There had been a great deal of blood on the lace curtains the night of the White Murders. Now that she thought of it, the county historian wasn't sure what had happened to those curtains or to any of the rest of the furnishings. Might they have been stored in an attic or a basement, waiting for someone to live in the house again and reclaim them?

The historian thought for a moment about what the curtains had witnessed and about their long years waiting with their secrets in a dark room. She thought long, dark, unclean thoughts . . . and then swore to snap herself out of it. Spooking herself was stupid. The Duncans were young; no doubt they had excellent nerves. They'd been told exactly what they were getting into, so they must be brave enough to bear it. If they were cheap besides—cheap enough to recycle murderous furnishings—that was their business.

It was the town's business too, of course, but the Duncans were newcomers and would find that out in time.

WEEKS PASSED. THE Duncans were seen in town now and then, never shopping (the merchants grumbled) but taking their time strolling the autumn streets. The town was at its loveliest at that time of year, all the oaks, maples, and sassafrases ablaze with color, the days crisp but clear and the nights cold enough for hot buttered rum. The cracker-barrel philosophers moved indoors to hold forth by the woodstoves. Children played noisy games in great piles of fallen leaves. Halloween decorations—on private front doors, in shop windows, on the long sloping lawns of schools—added to the festive air.

Old Ben Haverstick, who lived near the town cemetery, reported seeing the couple there one evening while he was walking his dog. The shadows were lengthening, the sunlight was dying, and no sensible adult went into a cemetery at that hour. Yet the Duncans were strolling that one at perfect leisure, walking arm in arm. A sudden gust of chilly wind carried young Mrs. Duncan's laughter to where Mr. Haverstick stood watching. It was silvery-sweet, like tiny bells, pretty as a china painting, and it froze his blood.

The couple were also seen visiting the library, haunting the oldest, dustiest stacks. Mrs. Parkinson, head librarian since time out of mind, told the other Daughters of the American Revolution all about their latest visit at that night's meeting. The Duncans, she said, had asked to see whatever records she had on the old rectory. There weren't many—blueprints, tradesmen's bills, a few fading church records written in cramped copperplate—but the couple seemed to be pleased. When she'd left them, young Mr. Duncan had been copying something into a small pocket notebook.

Most peculiar of all, the Duncans were never seen driving. Rectory House was in the country, though town had crept closer and closer over the years, and it was a long, slow hike over rolling hills from there to town. Yet the couple had no vehicle that anyone could see, and they never called Amos for cab rides. They simply appeared here and there from time to time, walking casually, giving no sign of being either footsore or spent. No one could remember seeing them come, let alone go; they were there, and then they weren't. It was very odd.

At this time, Missy Coffin, who edited the weekly *Gazette*, decided to write that year's Halloween story about the new owners of Rectory House. When she saw them walking in town, she asked to call on them.

The Duncans would be delighted to receive Ms. Coffin at any time, young Mrs. Duncan said, even though Ms. Coffin preferred to be received in the daytime. "The house is as harmless at night as it is by day," Mrs. Duncan had told her reassuringly.

Missy was not reassured by the way the woman had put it but set a day and time for the visit. Specifically, a day time. Everyone knew that nothing bad could happen by day.

MISSY COFFIN CLIMBED the hill to Rectory House on a cold morning after a night of frost. Before she went to the door, she took a few photos. The photos would run in the *Gazette* as grayscale halftones, but she thought the contrast might show through in grayscale: the brilliant leaves of the sugar maples and hawthornes against the stark, forbidding house. It was decaying—ancient paint was peeling off the clapboards, and some of the window glass appeared to be too brittle for modern use—but the faint air of vacancy that still hung about it added to the mystique. Missy hoped that the mystique would show through in the photos too.

There was no doorbell. The knocker which she saw before her was brightly polished and looked almost blacksmith-new; it was in a curious shape that Missy couldn't identify. Perhaps a cross? She was making a note to find out when the door opened (she hadn't knocked yet!) and Mrs. Duncan welcomed her in.

For a fraction of a fraction of a moment, she thought she saw right through Mrs. Duncan—all the way down the front hall into what looked like a parlor. But the illusion vanished as soon she stepped across the threshold. She didn't know that she was the first living person to enter the house in well over seventy years.

No one ever saw the Duncans or Missy Coffin again.

MISSY'S HALLOWEEN STORY about Rectory House—neatly typed and double-spaced, with her own characteristic typos—was dropped through the mail slot at the *Gazette* office the night before press day. Publisher Muriel Haverstick (who was publisher by virtue of being Old Ben's daughter-in-law) read the manuscript. When she finished, she read it over again, this time with a blue pencil. Then she walked it down to the printer's to have it set in type for the front page.

Missy's story was short and simple: The Duncans were ghosts (of course). Which explained a lot. Because the town was so curious about them, the town was invited to an open house at Rectory House on Halloween night. If any townspeople didn't believe in ghosts, the story said, they would before the night was through.

ON THE NIGHT of October 31, torches burned outside Rectory House. The house was dark. The line to get in was long. Most of those waiting were dressed in Halloween costumes under heavy coats and mufflers. An enterprising fellow sold spiced cider, hot chocolate, and popcorn out of his panel truck; he had steady, profitable trade.

Several bloggers were waiting to get in, along with a few stringers for area weeklies. No reporters from major media outlets showed up, on the grounds that the story was highly dubious, overly colored, a probable prank. This sort of thing was fine for the Internet and the weekly shoppers, the news directors said, but it wasn't news.

Also in attendance were ghost hunters from around the region, plus psychic mediums, paranormal psychologists, and a woman dressed like a movie gypsy who said she was a devil whisperer. That might not have been news either, but it could have made an amusing human-interest feature.

The open house was scheduled to start at midnight sharp. Town officials arrived at ten of.

The real estate agent surrendered the keys to Officer Frazier, who handed them to Deputy Crane, who formally presented them to Cyrus Heppleworth, mayor of the town. Mayor Heppleworth made a brief statement, acknowledged the applause, and posed for photos of himself unlocking the front door. The photo op was repeated until everyone who wanted the shot had it. Then the mayor stood back to let the ghost hunters, psychics, pararnormalists, minor media, and general public into the house.

No one ever came out again. Rectory House closed the next morning for good.

"WELL?" MISSY COFFIN demanded.

Her friends shifted nervously in their chairs around her kitchen table. Friends they might be, but this was tricky.

"So? What did you think?"

Eye met guilty eye around the room. Ben Haverstick (neither old nor anyone's father-in-law) flipped through the manuscript again, pretending to reread something. His cousin Muriel pretended to reread it with him. Cy Heppleworth, who'd finished his hot buttered rum before the end of Part 2, wished for more rum. Mrs. Parkinson's daughter, Polly, doodled on an inside page of the script. Dexter White's construction firm owned a couple of backhoes, and he knew that Missy knew it; he gave her very dirty looks when she wasn't looking.

Rectory House, the title page said. *A Haunting Halloween Tale*, it added.

"Did you get the *Macbeth* jokes?" the author asked.

They were obvious, unmissable, silly, but Missy was looking at Muriel, who realized that she'd have to say something. She cleared her throat to buy time before speaking. "You left out the weird sisters."

"No, I didn't. They were the witches."

A long pause followed, during which everyone absolutely refused to ask *Which witches?*

"Screw you guys," Missy snarled. "You didn't even think it was scary?"

Polly couldn't help it. "Only the writing."

The next long pause lasted longer but ended in raucous laughter. Missy started it.

"Gotcha," she told them. "Trick or treat. Good one, huh?"

Good one, the others agreed, relieved. And there was more hot buttered rum after that after all.

NO ONE QUITE remembered whose idea it was, but at some point during the last round, they decided to pay a call on Rectory House. How better to find out whether the stories were true? The house *did* have that bad reputation, but they'd all go together. Surely nothing could happen if they stuck together.

The six friends piled into Dex's big crew-cab pickup truck, eager for the adventure. He was too drunk to drive, and the others were too drunk to ride, but they were all well past caring. For fun, Muriel told them "The Hook" and "It's Coming from Inside the House" on the way.

They all wished she hadn't, of course, when they were on the doorstep of the terrible house.

No one wanted to go in first. Finally, Ben did. Polly followed. Missy said she'd go last. She insisted.

No one noticed when the house's doors locked themselves. Only when they heard a small thump against a window did anyone look out, and only then did anyone scream.

Missy Coffin's pale face was pressed against the dark glass, a mask of inhuman rage. But the sound the mask was making was laughter.

THE FIVE WHO went in that night never came out, and the one who didn't was never seen again. Forever after, Rectory House was more haunted than before, and Missy Coffin—whatever and wherever she was—had the last laugh.

WEIRD SISTERS

MARGARITA, AZAZELLA, AND Natasha were sisters, which was bad enough, and they were witches. Being witches, they lived in a scary old house, cast wicked spells, and befriended black cats. They were ageless, immortal, eerie, and misunderstood.

The sisters had lived in Rectory House for many a decade, as peacefully as any relatives who shared a hearth could. Young Mr. and Mrs. Duncan had made some trouble when they'd visited last—their nephew and niece-in-law had always liked a little joke; they'd staged the so-called White Murders some time back to scare the locals—but they were safely home now, causing the usual pother in Manhattan.

There'd also been some mischief involving a girl editor, a Spell of Misdirection, and a silly Halloween story, but the girl had turned out to be one of them—a distant relation who'd been working on some long, slow-burn theory about news versus truth. Why she'd snapped when she did was none of their concern. Their secrets remained safe; the townsfolk were healthily afraid of Rectory House again, and it might be a generation before anyone dared to come knocking.

The problem was Natasha. She wanted a new consort. Not one of the bloodless wraiths who haunted the old churchyard, who were sad and unsatisfying. Not another of the endlessly passing shades on the old high street, mostly Colonial soldiers killed by redcoats and eternally bitter about foreigners. Definitely not a dead farmer, blacksmith, stableboy, or schoolmaster (though Margarita's Ichabod had been amusing for a while). No—she wanted a good warlock, a strong one, a strong man who liked a strong witch. Or so she told her sisters at teatime one frosty autumn day.

Azazella nearly spat oolong. "Strong? For *you*? Since when?"

"Don't be hateful."

"I'm not being hateful, sister."

"If this is about the solicitor again—"

Margarita hushed them before they could get back into it. The solicitor—one Ebenezer Feeney—claimed to be a warlock and charmed Natasha out of her dainty slippers many years ago. He courted her devotedly in a deep, resonant, oily voice that made the cats yowl, after which he fleeced her out of a few Spells of Power and the best silver tea tray before Azazella caught on and turned him into a toad. There were rumors that his law practice thrived all the same.

"He said the sweetest things to me," Natasha said. "I wish I had another man to say sweet things to me. A man with a heart and a soul and a dark secret and a passionate nature." Before Azazella could interrupt, she added, "*And* a face I could gaze at for days."

"Hush, sister," Margarita urged. "We have no need of that now. Have a biscuit."

Azazella started again to point out Natasha's folly, but Margarita kicked her under the tea table. Many things are best left unsaid, just as many wishes are better unwished.

BUT A WISH spoken aloud is a spell of its own. A few afternoons later, the stranger came knocking.

The knock was unusually loud in the deep stillness of Rectory House. The witches gathered before the dark glass to See who was outside before they answered the door.

"Oh, sisters!" Natasha cried. "Look how pretty!"

Azazella tsk-ed at her. "You can't call a man pretty, Tasha."

This one was, though, call him what you would. The witches gazed at him in the glass, marveling at the perfection of his features, his faultless grooming, his fine clothing. *Interesting*, Margarita thought. *Suspicious*, Azazella thought. *Pretty!*, thought Natasha.

"We'll let him in," Margarita said. "We'll see what he wants. Then I'll decide what to do."

"You mean 'We'll decide,' sister," Azazella told her.

The eldest witch drew herself up ominously. "I mean what I say. Don't make me remind you what happened the last time *you* decided a thing."

"It was only a backhoe, Margo."

"It was only a mess in the garden."

Azazella harrumphed and sputtered and started to talk back about what Margarita had eventually done with that schoolmaster of hers, but Natasha was already running to open the front door.

LIKE THE WORD or not, he *was* pretty. Jakob Marlinspike was blessed with exceptional beauty, with a silver tongue and charm that wouldn't quit, and though these qualities didn't add up to strong, exactly, or constitute soulfulness, they were good enough for Natasha. Even the witches' huge black tomcat Behemoth took to him, which was exceedingly rare; they were down to one cat now because Behemoth kept gobbling up the others.

Margarita and Azazella watched from the hall outside the parlor while the young couple courted over tea. The boy had been calling every afternoon for weeks, and it was December now, getting on for the Nativity.

"He loves her," Margarita said.

Her sister snorted. "He loves her not."

"Why not?"

"I can't say for certain yet. A hunch."

The eldest witch pondered gravely. Azie's hunches were as good as most witches' foresight and far better than the best human guess. Over the centuries, she'd seen many things coming long before anyone else, alive or dead. She'd warned *everyone* about that certain politician.

Still, Jakob seemed to be smitten with Natasha, and Natasha obviously cared for him. Her sisters could almost see why. For a mortal, he had none of the usual tics, twitches, and vices; he was as gentlemanly as a modern boy could be. He might have stepped out of the nineteenth century, in those black clothes and the old-fashioned cloak he favored. His hair was slightly longer than worn today, and he was nearly as pale as one of Natasha's wraiths, with a grave, slightly sorrowful expression that implied hidden depths, Edgar Allan Poe as latter-day pinup boy.

Azazella had liked Mr. Poe in his time (which had been too short) and began to see her younger sister's attraction to this mortal boy. Yet she also saw a danger in him, something not quite what it seemed. For that reason, she withheld her approval. Natasha didn't need it, but Azazella needed to give it.

As for Margarita, she was irresistibly reminded of one of her own old mortals—not the schoolmaster Ichabod or the brilliant Russian Master but a Civil War soldier, Union Army, as fine a man as the gods had ever created. Jeremiah lay in a military cemetery down the high street. His plot was on the path of the ghost soldiers' nightly parade, but he never marched with the others. He'd hated the war. In life, he marched out of step on purpose, cursed his vain boyish dreams of glory, and got himself shot at Appomattox the day before the truce. Ever after, he refused to come out of his grave, even for her. Poor boy. She still missed him at times.

So if Natasha wanted a tall, dark, mysterious, and pretty stranger, Margarita could not object. Still, that hunch of Azie's . . .

She drew her brows down, frowning, to peer at Jakob again. He felt her gaze and smiled a smile of surpassing charm.

Margarita felt the smile and lost her heart.

AZAZELLA TOOK LONGER to come around. She'd always been slow to warm to strangers, even in ordinary mortal life; their parents had worried that she would never marry. She hadn't, as it happened, but it hadn't mattered. Nothing mattered after you turned into a witch.

Natasha was in the kitchen warming the teapot one afternoon when Azazella passed by the parlor. Jakob saw her and called to her. "You don't like me," he added, "but you might if you'd give me a chance."

"What chance is that?" Azazella asked, suspicious.

"Come and see."

When Natasha returned a few minutes later, Azazella made a hasty excuse and fled the parlor, her pulse fluttering like so many tiny birds flying in heart-shaped patterns.

JAKOB MARLINSPIKE PROPOSED to Natasha the third Sunday afternoon of Advent. Being witches, the sisters didn't observe Christian festivals but knew about them all the same. Getting engaged so close to the Nativity seemed to be significant.

"He wants us to marry in the old stone church," Natasha said dreamily, "on Nativity Eve, after sunfall."

"You mean Solstice Eve, sister," Azazella corrected.

But Margarita hushed her. The boy was a Catholic, so-called, and Natasha could bow her knee to his faith long enough to wed him. After that, denomination would be inconsequential. In all supernatural belief systems, marriage was a bond, which made a Catholic ceremony no higher or lower than a Protestant one and neither inferior to the great pagan rites.

Natasha ran on, unheeding. She would wear a fine white Yule gown and a garland of winter flowers; she would have dainty crystal slippers and a lace train thirty feet long.

While she talked and talked, her sisters envied her joy in silence. More to the point, they envied her boy. Jakob was so attractive, so engaging, so *thrilling*. Margarita privately doubted that little Tasha could fully appreciate his charms—at least, not the way that a witch of the world could. Not the way *she* did . . . and often had.

More privately still, Azazella wished for another hour alone with the boy; she knew she could turn him to her forever if they had one more hour.

But because they loved their sister, they set aside their desires in favor of hers. A witch could never truly marry a mortal, but it would be cruel to deprive Natasha of her dream of wedlock. Each witch secretly decided to sacrifice the boy at the altar to seal the match. Then she'd work out how— and whether—to share his ghost.

AT SUNFALL ON Nativity Eve, the great stone cathedral was deserted. Mass would be celebrated at midnight; now the parishioners were home with their families, sharing their hopes for the coming day over their Nativity Eve dinners.

Four beings were in the sanctuary at that hour: the groom, Jakob Marlinspike, straight-backed and handsome in correct evening black, and three witches, all dressed in fine white Yule gowns from the Old World. Natasha had her thirty-foot train, her crystal slippers, the garland of winter flowers. Azazella, who was filling the dual roles of bridesmaid and best witch, carried a bouquet of thorns and thistles. And Margarita, the eldest, wore a grand cope of imperial purple over her gown; she would perform a pagan marriage ritual while dressed in a Catholic vestment, which all agreed would serve well enough.

There was no book on the altar. There was no need for one.

"Do you take this man, sister?" Margarita asked Natasha.

Natasha said the words of the vow the young couple had chosen to exchange. "I take him now and forever, life beyond death and life everlasting," she said.

The young witch smiled into her mortal boy's eyes as she spoke, glowing with what might very well have been love, and her sisters knew pangs of regret. There could be no marriage between witches and mortals, they knew, but this foolish affair was so lovely somehow.

Margarita turned her attention from Jakob to seek Azazella's eyes. To her great surprise and even greater distress, Azazella was gazing at the boy much as his bride was doing.

"Sister!"

Azazella started guiltily, nearly dropping her bouquet. "What is it, sister?"

Margarita's expression answered the question. Azazella lowered her eyes in shame for a moment. When she looked up again, however, Margarita was mooning at the boy like a lovestruck cow.

"Sister!"

With a start, Margarita recalled herself. She would have to finish the rites, however she felt about them, because the sooner the wedding was over, the sooner she could kill the groom.

Furtively, she felt for the large curved knife that she'd hidden behind the altar.

"Jakob Marlinspike," she said, "do you take this witch, our beloved sister?"

The bridegroom bowed his head. "I take her life, now and forever, life beyond death and life everlasting. As God is my witness."

The sisters exchanged glances. That wasn't the vow they'd agreed on, and they'd definitely agreed to leave out the God part.

"As *we* are your witnesses," Margarita corrected, "as you are nearly our brother."

Unexpectedly, the boy dropped Natasha's hands. He took a step back from the altar. He smiled gently, gravely, charmingly.

"I think not," he said. "You are witches."

Azazella bristled. "See here, boy, you knew us for what we were before you made this compact with our sister." She glanced at Natasha, who was too shocked and surprised to cry yet but not too shocked to understand that something was going quite wrong.

"You are witches," he repeated, "all of you, and you know what happens to witches. I will not wed with your kind. Witches burn."

"It would take a better man than you to burn me, boy," Azazella growled, while Margarita glared, while Natasha burst into confused, frightened tears at the foot of the altar.

"It would," Jakob agreed, reaching into his pocket.

The crucifix was small, golden, and brilliant by candlelight. The witches blinked at it, uncertain what to do about it.

"In the name of the One who comes tonight," the boy said, holding the crucifix up to them, "in His name, I renounce you. I do this in return for forgiveness of the sins that would damn me forever."

Margarita, who was already reaching for the curved knife, began to laugh. "Oh, for love of the Dark, is *that* all?" She understood now that the boy had asked to marry in the church for what he thought would be protection.

Likewise, Azazella was smiling—rather wickedly. The boy might be seeking redemption, but she knew that his religion made no provision for redemption from what he'd done with her. She brought out the dagger that she'd concealed inside her bouquet.

Only Natasha saw no humor or opportunity for murder in the situation. She was certain that she loved Jakob and up until then had been certain that he loved her.

Jakob moved a few steps closer. "I renounce you all. I claim your lives as my prize."

"You speak nonsense," Margarita said calmly, raising the knife.

But the boy was unafraid, because he had the better weapon. (Not the crucifix.) "You thought me wise enough when you had me," he told her, "you and all your sisters alike."

For the space of a heartbeat, no one spoke or moved or drew breath.

Then the witches cast dreadful curses on one another—harmful spells, hurtful ones, spells that smoked and stung. But they saved the worst for Jakob Marlinspike. He went up in a pillar of flame, turned into a pillar of salt, then one of pepper, and back to salt before collapsing to ash.

FATHER O'MALLEY FOUND Jakob's crucifix in the ashes when he unlocked the church before Mass. He made the altar boys clean up the mess while he had a quick, reviving goblet of sacramental wine.

It appeared that the stories were true. Jakob Marlinspike, dead two hundred years, *did* come out of his grave and *did* walk the world when called. Whoever had called him, the priest hoped they regretted it now. The crucifix had been too hot to touch when the altar boys tried, and even now, the pail of cold water in which they'd placed it (with tongs) still boiled.

Resigned, Father O'Malley used a Latin incantation to send what was left of Jakob back underground. The priest knew that the troublemaking dead man would rise again, as evildoers do. But he would lie quiet until then.

BACK AT RECTORY House, the witches made the best peace they could. Margarita and Azazella blamed Natasha, who blamed them back, but mostly, they blamed Jakob Marlinspike. He wouldn't have taken them in, they said, had they only been colder and wiser. They vowed to be colder and wiser next time.

Malice, self-interest, and ignorance are weird sisters, never weirder than when they try to deny their kinship. But a man who turns sister on sister on sister is a man who ends badly.

More than once.

Note: The names of the sisters, and Behemoth the cat, come from Mikhail Bulgakov's *The Master and Margarita.*

SPOOK HOUSE

RECTORY HOUSE WAS empty again, even of witches. A year after Jakob Marlinspike rose from his grave to trick them, the witch sisters, still haunted by his memory, moved out. The townspeople were unaware that they'd ever moved in. Thanks to a few well-crafted Spells of Concealment, as far as anyone knew, the house had stood vacant for nearly a century, ever since the White Murders. But now Rectory House was well and truly alone except for stinging shadows and black things that brooded alone in the dark.

Margarita, Azazella, and Natasha had cursed it before they left to make sure that no one would ever live in it again.

Unluckily, however, Natasha's bit of the spell went a little wrong. No one would ever live in the house again, but nothing said the house itself couldn't live.

Rectory House decided that it wanted to do exactly that. It was alive now, and waiting.

THE FIRST SPIRIT to visit was a Minuteman from the old military cemetery, who'd taken a wrong turn after stepping out of the dead soldiers' parade on the high street. He'd had no earthly need to leave the parade—he had no biological functions—but his ghost still enjoyed peeing on trees.

He'd gone deeper into the woods than usual that night in search of a good tree. After he discharged his needless task (on a nice black locust), he started back for the high street. But ten minutes' wandering in the woods took him nowhere. He was beginning to think he was lost.

Only then did he see the house in the clearing, ghostly by moonlight. It appeared to be deserted. At any rate, an air of long neglect hung about it. Its once-white paint was peeling; its once-green shutters had faded to a murky, indeterminate color; the brick chimneys were crumbling. But the longer he looked at the house, the more alive it seemed and the better he liked it. He peered through a downstairs window before opening the door (which was unlocked) and stepping over the threshold.

THE HOUSE SMILED, licked its chops, and locked the door.

THREE NIGHTS LATER, a ghostly woman appeared in the clearing, standing where the Minuteman had stood. In life, they'd been married. In practice, he'd been faithless. Still, she'd loved him and hated being without him even now. Until that week, they'd slept side by side undisturbed for centuries, the carving on their headstone weathered now to illegibility and only weeds decorating their graves.

She was a Virginian by way of Essex, a planter's daughter who'd defied her family to run off with a poor man, and she'd taken her stubborn nature with her into the afterworld. Faithful or not, he'd been her husband, and death would not part them.

Three midnights after he never came back from the parade on the high street, she left their plot to find him, tracking his path through the woods to the place where it stopped. The moonlight drew her eye to an abandoned house that might have been a ghost itself.

It was no Virginia planter's mansion or even the small, drafty frame house where she'd passed her married life. But the old Colonial had clearly been a fine home in its day, and she saw beauty even in its ruins.

While she stood there admiring the slant of the roof, the shade of her husband's shade appeared in an upstairs window. She knew it was doubly dead because it was transparent to her. The vision lasted a mortal heartbeat or two; then it vanished.

She should have been frightened. The ghost of a ghost couldn't possibly be a thing that a ghost would want to meet. But she was stubborn and Southern, and whatever had been in the window, she was married to it. So she approached slowly over the weedy grounds, watching the window where she'd seen the apparition.

The house seemed to smile at her. As she drew near, the front door swung open. To her surprise, it opened smoothly and quietly on its hinges, as though they'd been newly oiled.

Gathering up her skirts, she stepped over the threshold. The door swung shut behind her, and the bolt shot soundlessly into its frame.

She had a few seconds left to think that somehow, she'd come home.

THAT WAS THE start of it. For weeks on end, drawn by an impulse they couldn't identify, ghosts flocked to the house from all over town: soldiers of the Continental Army, Civil War bluecoats, farmers and teachers and blacksmiths, butchers and bakers and candlestick makers, pretty maids all in a row. Some were buried in the old churchyard behind the house. Others lay in the old cemeteries around town. None of those who entered the house came out again.

No living person saw—in mortal eyes, Rectory House was still abandoned—but the house appeared to grow younger with each new ghost it took in. The white clapboards repainted themselves; the green shutters regreened; the brick chimneys rebricked. At the same time, the house grew larger, as though to accommodate an expanding population of resident spirits.

Then the day came when the house began changing its character entirely. Slowly but surely, it went Southern. Its white clapboards turned pale lemon yellow; a gallery with sky-blue ceilings and overhead fans encircled it; live oaks drove out the sugar maples and hawthornes on the grounds, which were weedless now and well-groomed. Large plate-glass windows smiled charmingly over the gallery railings.

No Yankee, living or dead, had ever seen such a thing at that latitude. The house absolutely didn't go with snow, autumn color, hot cider, or roasted chestnuts. It was made for long hot humid summers, frosty juleps, ice cubes clinking in tumblers of bourbon, dancing fireflies at night. It was as foreign to Yankee ghosts as a drawl, as irresistible as a Carolina belle, and it attracted dead men (and women) from across the county.

None of them ever returned.

The house was still growing; perhaps it was still hungry. Most evenings now, mortals who lived near the high street swore they smelled smoke.

FINALLY, ONE DARK moonless night, Jakob Marlinspike's ghost came back to Rectory House. Something had drawn him there, though he couldn't say what. If he remembered the witch sisters, he gave no sign.

Natasha's curse remembered, however. It opened the door and welcomed him in.

Jakob never saw it coming. No ghost who entered Rectory House did. There was a scream. There was silence. There was no more Jakob.

There were no ghosts at all to hear the witchly laughter.

The windows watched—brilliant, alert, alive—over the gallery railings, still smiling charmingly, waiting for the next visitor. What came out of the chimneys wasn't woodsmoke; it painted pale, shifting patterns on the black sky.

EPILOGUE
DAY TRAIN

DAY WAS ON the horizon when Clara finished her stories. By now, the sky was shot through with faint pinks and golds, and the first early trains were running on the opposite track. Soon, her train would pass the coffee roastery, which would be open again after the holiday, and the car would fill with wonderful smells. That was why she rode the last run of the *Midnight Limited*. Coffee was beyond her power to drink now, but it was still redolent of morning and youth and vital, joyous life. Preemptively, she cracked the window.

The boy leaned across her to close it. He'd been shivering most of the night. What monster opened windows on a freezing-cold train in January in a Northern town?

Clara cared nothing for his discomfort. He was new; he still thought he felt things. She reopened the window, this time wider.

He reclosed it.

They did this a few more times.

Finally, she slammed the window all the way open and warned him that his next try would be his last.

He said he wasn't scared of her. She said nothing. He moved across the aisle (to a seat next to a closed window) and sulked for a while in silence. When he spoke again, it was only to report that the sun was coming up. Still, she said nothing.

"I said, the *sun's* coming up. Don't we have to get off the train?"

"And go where?"

"Somewhere. Don't we?"

"Don't you?"

He didn't hear or maybe didn't bother to listen; he was checking his antique pocket watch. "Look, I *know* we have to get off. *Midnight Limited* stops at quarter till. *Downtown Zephyr* starts on the hour. It's twenty till now. Where do we go in the daytime?"

"Wherever I want."

That, the boy heard. He frowned. "A little help here? Where do we go?"

The brick bulk of the roastery loomed ahead, lights burning in some of its windows; Clara could already smell the coffee. She put her head out the open window and extended her tongue to taste the air.

"What now?" the boy insisted.

She didn't answer until she'd breathed her fill. At last, she pulled her head back into the car, closed the window, and dusted her coat front. The first glints of sunlight struck her gilded buttons as she stood.

"Come with me," Clara said.

The boy who looked like Cyril followed her. When they reached the door she'd pushed him out of earlier, he started to get it and started to run, but she was too fast.

She watched his body skip down the opposite track like a rock; then she watched the milk train run over it. Something transparent oozed over the rails. He was dead again.

That was almost as good as caffeine. Not as good as killing Cyril's ghost would be someday.

He still had it coming. He'd had a second, secret engagement to Rose Lovejoy when he'd gone off to that damned war in Cuba a secret she learned six weeks after his death, the shock that drove her to jump off the trolley. She hadn't seen his ghost yet, not in all this time. But she was patient. She knew he'd come back to this city—their town—eventually. He'd ride this train—their trolley—in good time. She could wait.

Meanwhile, all this practice would make perfect.

She stood in the open door of the car dreaming of revenge, luxuriating in delicious anticipation. Cyril still loved her; she knew it. He'd come back to her someday. She'd let him.

And then . . . and then . . .

And then the ghost of the boy whose ghost she'd killed ten minutes earlier pushed her off the train.

He watched Clara fall, bounce, splatter, devolve into transparent goo. Now *she* was dead again.

All that long night, she'd made him listen to her terrible stories of vengeance, so she'd had it coming. But now that he'd killed her back, it would be her turn again. And so on and so on, maybe forever. If death didn't stick, and evidently it didn't, the two of them might be locked into afterlives of endless two-way murder—a prospect that should have sickened him but did not. In fact, he found that he was looking forward to it.

Revenge is a fast train that never stops. Not even for the dead.

K. Simpson was once described as "a surprisingly affable Devil-worshipper," none of which is true.